Sex, Lies, and Sugar

ELLA SPENCER

Sex, Lies, and Sugar

For the couples.

Chapter 1

Palm Springs, California, 1969—a world of sleek mid-century modern architecture, smooth lines, and an aura of effortless sophistication. The Old Las Palmas neighborhood, one of the most wealthy and exclusive neighborhoods in Palm Springs, welcomed a unique procession of women. Emerging from their pristine homes, these women were the epitome of the era's charm and style.

Kitty Bloom, a voluptuous blonde with a penchant for tight capri pants and cleavage-revealing tops, strutted confidently. Her attire, a vivid turquoise, complemented her flamboyant personality, accentuated by an abundance of jewelry. Kitty carried a casserole, wrapped meticulously, an offering for the gathering.

Marybelle Beedum, a petite brunette with a striking resemblance to Louise Brooks, followed. Dressed in a chic Paco Rabanne bathing suit, her look was softened by a delicate chiffon coverlet. Marybelle's quiet demeanor contrasted with her extraordinary appearance, making her a captivating presence.

Florene Johnson, the epitome of glamour, donned a two-piece Pucci bathing suit, her look completed with sparkling diamonds. Her beauty, reminiscent of a classic movie star, turned heads wherever she went. Florene carried herself with a confidence that spoke of a life lived in the spotlight.

Jerome Holleran, the outlier, embraced a more androgynous style. Her butter-colored seersucker suit gave her a dashing appearance. Jerome's presence added a layer of intrigue to the group, her masculine elegance setting her apart.

Together, the women walked down the sunlit street, their brightly colored hats bouncing with each step. The sound of their high heels echoed on the pavement, a rhythmic prelude to their gathering.

They arrived at Sugar Bainbridge's luxurious ranch-style estate, a home that was the epitome of Palm Springs chic. The sprawling property boasted clean lines, expansive glass windows, and an aura of opulence. As the doorbell chimed, Sugar, a great beauty with a model's body, opened the door with a radiant smile.

"Hi, ladies, come on in!" she greeted, her voice warm and welcoming.

Inside Sugar's kitchen, a hub of social activity, the women began to share their culinary creations. Kitty, eager to impress, presented her dish with pride. "I love how French it sounds. En papillote. I just made Potted Meat Bernadette."

Jerome, ever the skeptic, glanced at the dish. "It's just a piece of paper."

Sugar, always the gracious hostess, smiled. "I wanted to try something new."

The women exchanged glances; their competitive spirits subtly masked by polite conversation. Marybelle, holding her dish, offered a modest smile. "Just dessert. Probably won't be as good as yours."

Kitty, not one to miss an opportunity for a culinary critique, set her casserole dish on the counter. "Now be nice, but I tried something new. I used that meat spread with the little devil on the front..."

Florene, curious, grabbed a fork and tasted it. "Do you even know what's in that stuff?"

Kitty shrugged. "And instead of using flour and milk, I just plopped in two cans of Cream of Mushroom. You were so right, Sugar."

Kitty remembered the two women laughing over the solidified soup, a testament to their shared sense of humor and experimentation.

Kitty flipped through a magazine, stopping at a particular photo. "Florene? Is that you?"

Florene nodded, a hint of pride in her eyes.

Marybelle blushed. "My Lord, you can almost see your—"

Jerome interrupted with a smirk. "Nope, not almost. You can definitely see it."

Kitty curiously leaned in. "How do you do it?"

Florene smiled, her eyes twinkling with mystery. "It's a secret."

Sugar, always conscious of her appearance, sighed. "I need to diet."

Jerome shook her head. "No, you don't."

The sun-drenched desert afternoon continued as the women relaxed around the pool on chaise lounges, each soaking up the golden rays. The scene was a tableau of modern glamor. Plates stacked with wedges of their various dishes sat within arm's reach, evidence of their shared culinary indulgence.

Jerome leaned back into her chaise, her expression

thoughtful. "I don't know. You know Leslie is just so content or... What's the word?"

"He's a sweetheart," Sugar offered, her voice light.

Jerome shook her head, a hint of frustration in her tone. "No, he's weak-willed. He just accepts it all."

Kitty chimed in, "I'm of the belief that what you say out loud becomes your reality."

Jerome rolled her eyes, her voice dripping with sarcasm. "Oh, stick it, Kitty."

Florene, lounging with the grace of a queen, changed the subject. "You ever read *Miss Lonelyhearts*?"

Marybelle, distracted, examined her reflection in a compact mirror. "Do my eyes look gray? Do I have gray eyes?"

Florene ignored her, continuing, "It's a good book."

Marybelle, still fixated on her reflection, frowned. "I look like an animal."

With a smirk, Florene teased, "Honey, I'd act like an animal if I had that husband of yours."

Marybelle ignored the comment, focusing on adjusting her hair. The playful banter continued.

Suddenly, Sugar jumped up, her energy infectious. "Jesus, it's Armageddon out here. Let's mix up some daiquiris."

Jerome smirked. "You can skip the lime and just bring me the rum, Shug."

Inside Sugar's luxurious kitchen, the blender whirred to life, mixing up a batch of daiquiris. The air was filled with the scent of fresh limes and rum, a heady mix that promised a carefree afternoon.

As the blender stopped, Sugar poured the drinks, her thoughts seemingly far away. "Talking about Marybelle's husband got me thinking."

Florene quipped, "I knew it would."

"Shut up," Sugar shot back with a playful grin. "I was thinking, why don't we have a potluck Sunday night? With none of our husbands going to work Monday because of the holiday, it might be a nice change."

Jerome, leaning against the counter, looked slightly put out. "Do our other halves have to come?"

Sugar nodded, her eyes gleaming with mischief. "Of course. But to make it more exciting, we could make it a contest. Each of us brings a dish, and the men can vote."

Kitty looked uncertain. "I don't know."

Marybelle modestly sighed. "I can't win against you all..."

Jerome, her eyes lighting up with the prospect of a challenge, grinned. "Thank God, finally some action around here. I have a trick or two up my sleeve."

Sugar raised an eyebrow, teasingly. "You have a trick or two up your pant leg."

Florene declared, "Ladies, the war is on." She extended her hand, a gesture of unity and competition. The others followed suit, placing their hands atop hers, with Marybelle hesitantly joining last.

The moment was charged with anticipation and camaraderie, as the women prepared for their culinary showdown. As they cheered, each woman carried her own secrets, desires, and dreams, all wrapped in a glamorous facade.

Chapter 2

The sun beat down on the serene neighborhood, casting glowing hues across the pristine homes and lush desert flora. The air was filled with the scent of blooming flowers, mingling with the aroma of freshly baked dishes. The immaculate front doors of the homes opened in unison, each revealing a perfectly curated scene of domestic elegance.

Kitty Bloom, radiant in a vibrant floral dress, emerged from her house, carrying a casserole dish with a confident flair. Her husband, Sterling, dressed in a sharp suit that accentuated his polished demeanor, walked beside her, casting a warm, protective shadow.

Across the street, Jerome and Leslie Holleran exited their home, waving cheerfully. Jerome wore a bright white suit, her stride confident and assured. Leslie exuded a quiet warmth, though his eyes held a hint of shyness.

As the couples made their way to the ultra-luxurious Bainbridge estate, the desert heat seemed to amplify the vibrant colors of their outfits. Sugar's home, an architectural marvel, contrasted beautifully with the rich, earthy tones of the desert.

At the door, Conrad Bainbridge, tall and charismatic,

greeted them with a martini in hand. His presence was magnetic, his smile broad and inviting. "Hello, neighbors!" he called out, his voice warm and welcoming. "Come on in. The old lady's upstairs fixing up."

Kitty and Sterling exchanged pleasantries, while Jerome gave Conrad a light punch on the arm. "Good to see you, Conny," she said with a grin.

Conrad grinned back, his eyes twinkling with mischief. "You make a beautiful man, Jerome," he teased, drawing a chuckle from her. As Conrad's gaze shifted to Leslie, he extended an invitation with characteristic ease. "Hey, do you golf? You should come play some holes with Sterling and me sometime."

Leslie hesitated, clearly taken aback, but Conrad's friendly insistence left little room for refusal. "Well, I—"

"Great. Let's play tomorrow. Pick you up at nine," Conrad concluded, his tone definitive.

The doorbell chimed again, heralding the arrival of Marybelle and Max Beedum. Marybelle, petite and striking, was a vision of charm. The couple greeted everyone warmly.

Inside the cool, sophisticated interior of the house, the guests gathered in the front room, where a bar was set up with crystal decanters and glasses. Jerome handed Leslie a martini with a playful grin. "Leslie, you're on bar duty. Make mine eight to one," she quipped, winking.

"Hey, why don't you all fix up some martinis and I'll go get the old ball and chain. Be down in two shakes," Conrad excused himself to fetch Sugar, leaving the guests to enjoy the casual elegance of the gathering.

Upstairs, in the privacy of their bedroom, Sugar stood

before her vanity, applying the finishing touches to her makeup. Her reflection revealed a stunning woman, her beauty accentuated by the soft glow of the room's lighting.

From the bathroom, Conrad's voice carried a hint of irritation. "You've been messing with my stuff," he accused.

Sugar sighed, not turning to face him. "Not tonight, Conny. We have company."

Conrad's frown deepened. "My tweezers are upside down. You been using them on your eyebrows? There's fucking hair on it." His voice was gruff, laced with annoyance as he flushed the toilet and walked into the room, holding his grooming set.

"Don't touch my fucking shit. You know better than that," he muttered, placing the kit back in his bedside drawer.

As he passed Sugar, he gave her a hard smack on the ass, more forceful than playful. Sugar flinched, her expression momentarily wounded as she set her lipstick down on the dresser. The moment was fleeting, but it left a mark, a subtle crack in the façade of their seemingly perfect life.

Returning downstairs, Sugar joined her guests, her radiant smile firmly in place. The room was alive with laughter and the clinking of glasses. As she handed out drinks and ensured everyone was comfortable, she felt the familiar pull of her role as the life of the party. The evening promised to be a success, filled with good food, lively conversation, and the unspoken competition of who could outshine whom in this small circle of friends.

The men, gathered in the front room, continued their conversation. Sterling looked Max up and down, "Max, you're looking fit. You been working out?"

"Man, just, you know, running and messing a little with the weights," Max replied modestly.

Sterling smiled, "Love to join you sometime. I feel the paunch coming on."

Max laughed, promising to share his workout secrets. Meanwhile, Leslie quietly mixed drinks, his introverted nature contrasting sharply with the more boisterous personalities around him.

As the doorbell rang once more, Max opened it to greet Florene and Burt Johnson. "Burt!" Max exclaimed, shaking hands warmly.

"Maximillian!" Burt replied with equal enthusiasm. Florene, stunning as always, smiled graciously.

"Wow! Florene," Max raised his eyebrows, "you look fantastic."

"Thanks, *dahling*," Florene responded, kissing Max's cheek. "Where are the ladies?" she inquired.

"Kitchen," Max directed her, and Florene made her way there. Sterling, still holding court in the front room, turned to Leslie. "Leslie, you still working over at the University?"

Before Leslie could respond, Jerome interjected playfully, "Yep, he's still answering the President's phone," she teased.

Leslie handed Sterling a martini. Sterling took a sip and grimaced slightly. "I like mine a little dirtier," he remarked, prompting Leslie to turn back to the bar and add more olive juice.

Chapter 3

From the window, the sunset bathed the women in a warm glow as they gathered around the kitchen counter, each cradling a martini in one hand. The room buzzed with a mix of anticipation and light-hearted chatter, the kind that fills a room with comfort and camaraderie. Jerome sat perched on the countertop, her legs swinging casually as she took a sip from her glass.

"When I was five," Jerome began, her voice carrying a hint of amusement, "my mother told me I was adopted and then she handed me a bucket and some cleaning supplies and said, 'Now, get to work.' That was the beginning of my life as a poet."

Her words hung in the air, drawing curious glances from the other women. Jerome's tone was playful, yet there was an underlying current of sincerity that caught their attention. Sugar, who had just entered the kitchen, paused to listen, a curious smile playing on her lips.

"I wrote my first poem that day," Jerome continued, her eyes closing momentarily as she recalled the memory. "I still have it. I scribbled it on a piece of toilet paper during a break from scrubbing the pot."

Jerome's voice softened, taking on a lyrical quality. "Dreams are candy. And mothers are dark smears on

17

white porcelain," she recited, opening her eyes to meet the gazes of her friends. "I wrote a poem every single day. One poem for every day of my life. I wrote while polishing the silver or washing the dishes or hanging the laundry out on the line. I wrote as I cleaned the vomit off the carpet after one of mother's nightly binges. Let's just say that I lived in the perfect environment for a poet to thrive."

With a graceful hop, she slid off the counter, her words leaving a contemplative silence in their wake.

Kitty, unable to grasp Jerome's cryptic storytelling, frowned slightly. "What the hell is she talking about? She doesn't even know what a poem is."

Florene, always ready with a quip, smirked and took a sip of her drink. "She's getting her stories from the bottle," she remarked, her voice dripping with sarcasm.

Jerome grinned mischievously. "Started early!" she declared, raising her glass in a mock toast.

The moment was broken by Marybelle, who reached over to turn on the radio. The last strains of a swinging tune filled the air, but they were quickly interrupted by a news report.

"Yesterday, movie legend Judy Garland was found dead in the bathroom of her rented Chelsea, London house," the announcer's voice intoned solemnly.

"Shit," Jerome muttered, her playful demeanor fading.

Sugar's eyes widened in shock. "Good Lord," she whispered, her hand going to her mouth.

The announcer continued, detailing the circumstances of Garland's death and the tragic decline that preceded it. "Garland had turned 47 just 12 days prior to her death. Her Wizard of Oz co-star Ray Bolger commented, saying, 'She just plain wore out.'"

"47? That's too young," Kitty murmured, her voice tinged with sadness.

Marybelle, usually so composed, looked visibly shaken. "It's too bad, just too bad."

Leslie, who had been quiet until now, spoke up, his voice filled with melancholy. "We saw her at Carnegie Hall," he said, his eyes distant as he recalled the memory. Jerome, sensing his distress, gave his hand a comforting squeeze. A soft, mournful tune played on the radio, a tribute to Garland's legacy.

The room fell silent, each person lost in their own thoughts. The news had cast a pall over the gathering, a reminder of the fragility of life and the fleeting nature of fame.

Conrad entered the room, breaking the silence with his usual bravado. "Is it time to eat yet?" he called out, his voice cutting through the somber atmosphere.

The couples made their way to the dining room, where a buffet of casseroles awaited. The dishes, lined up neatly on the sideboard, were a testament to the women's culinary skills, though their pallid, glutinous appearance left much to be desired.

Sugar addressed her guests with a flirtatious and serious tone. "My friends, here it is, the first round of what will be many—"

"Burt interrupted her, his voice stammering with excitement. "Cuh-cuh-casserole wars," he declared, eliciting a round of stifled laughter from the men.

Sugar, holding up a T-shirt with "Queen Casserole" emblazoned on it, announced the prize for the best dish. "The inventors of the favorite dish of the evening will receive this groovy T-shirt."

Conrad chimed in, "And for the lucky S.O.B. married to her?"

Kitty raised a matching "King Casserole" tee, her eyes sparkling with mischief.

Leslie shared a memory. "My father gave me a T-shirt for my fifth birthday that read 'Daddy's Little Question Mark,'" he said, his voice tinged with nostalgia.

"Why can't we just have a dinner party? I hate this competition stuff," Kitty complained.

Jerome shot back, "That's because deep down inside you know you won't win."

"Jerome!" Kitty protested, but her tone was more playful than offended.

Sterling reassured his wife. "It's okay, babe. She's just jealous you're a better cook."

Max, glancing at the TV, scoffed at the commercial playing for Tang. "Dehydrated food and powders. I'm supposed to believe an astronaut can survive on Tang?" he remarked, his tone dripping with skepticism.

Florene, visibly hungry, chimed in, "Get with the words, I want food."

Burt nodded in agreement, "Florene's hungry. We better get on with it."

Sugar, sensing the anticipation, stood up with a playful yet authoritative air. "What do you say? Is everybody ready?"

The group responded in unison, "Yes ma'am," their voices a mix of excitement and mock seriousness.

Everyone stiffened, holding their forks upright in a mock display of disciplined eagerness.

"On your mark," Sugar announced, her voice teasingly dramatic.

The diners, eyes serious and forks vibrating with

anticipation, leaned forward.

"Get set," she continued, drawing out the suspense.

And then, with a flourish, she shouted, "Go!"

In an instant, they pounced from their seats, rushing toward the buffet with the energy and excitement of kids at a candy store.

The urgency of the moment driving them to pile their plates high with the unappetizing concoctions. The scene was a mix of grotesque and humorous, the diners attacking the food with a fervor that belied its questionable quality.

Marybelle, eager to impress, described her dish. "I soaked the chicken livers in Armagnac before folding them in at the end," she explained, her voice filled with pride.

The guests ate with gusto, their mouths tearing into the stringy meat and gelatinous textures. The sound of forks scraping plates, and the occasional grunt or moan of satisfaction filled the air. The scene was a tableau of excess, a celebration of indulgence in all its messy glory.

Leslie, ever the movie buff, drew a parallel to a classic film. "Remember in 'All About Eve' when Bette Davis bites into that raw green onion? I am currently having the same experience," he quipped, eliciting a round of laughter.

The room buzzed with the sound of indulgence— grunts, moans, and the eager gulping of wine. It was a scene of pure gluttony, everyone absorbed in their meals.

"I don't know, I feel a lot better if I line the pan with foil. Call it a quirk," Kitty mentioned, focused on her cleaning.

"I don't think it browns as evenly with the foil. I've had better luck just greasing the pan," Sugar offered, sharing her culinary insight.

"Why do they call it OLEO? When it is margarine? What in the hell is OLEO?" Max questioned, puzzled by the terminology.

"I love potato chips on tuna. I really do," Burt declared, unashamed of his preference.

"That's mine, baby. That's my tuna!" Jerome responded quickly, taking pride in her dish.

"Is pimiento a vegetable?" Marybelle asked, still unsure.

"It's a pepper," Sugar clarified, keeping the conversation light.

"A pepper? Oh no, it can't be," Marybelle replied, still in disbelief.

"I really thought Dr. Pepper was a real person but it turns out, he's not," Leslie added, seemingly out of nowhere.

"Big piece of gristle in this one," Conrad muttered, taking a jab at Sugar's dish, which she felt sharply.

"I couldn't personally eat sweetbreads. It's the brains, right?" Kitty continued, changing the subject.

"No. Pancreas or thymus," Max corrected her.

"God, a pancreas is a heavy-duty internal organ," Burt noted, intrigued.

"Really? What's a thymus?" Florene asked, curious.

"It's a gland in your neck, no, hah, in the calf's neck," Jerome explained with a laugh.

"Oh no, not a calf. God, how horrible. I could never eat a baby," Marybelle exclaimed, horrified at the thought.

Sugar, sensing an opportunity for levity, interjected with a sly smile. "Baby? Don't you have a baby? Florene, am I wrong? I'm sorry to change the subject, but you do have a baby? I distinctly remember you having a baby."

Florene, her expression enigmatic, confirmed Sugar's question. "Oh, yes, I did. I had a baby. I don't know what happened. I sat him down one day and I never saw him again."

The room fell silent, the revelation hanging in the air like a cloud. The guests exchanged uncomfortable glances, unsure of how to respond.

Florene's mind drifted back to that day, a hazy memory brought into sharp focus. She remembered the party, the laughter and music, the feel of the sun on her skin. She had been holding her fussy baby, trying to juggle him and her cigarette. The baby had been crying incessantly, and in a moment of frustration, she had put him down and walked away. The image of his tiny body crawling toward the open door was etched in her mind, a ghostly reminder of that fleeting moment.

Marybelle's voice broke the silence. "That's just awful," she murmured, her eyes wide with disbelief.

Florene smiled, her expression inscrutable. Burt, ever the supportive husband, winked at her, his eyes twinkling with affection.

Conrad finished licking his plate clean and skeptically declared, "I don't believe a word of it."

As the guests leaned back in their chairs, sated and slightly tipsy, the atmosphere shifted. The initial excitement of the competition had given way to a more subdued, introspective mood. The evening had revealed more than just culinary skills—it had laid bare the complexities and contradictions of their lives, a tapestry of secrets, regrets, and unspoken desires.

Chapter 4

The atmosphere in Sugar's dining room was electric, filled with the anticipation of the night's big reveal. Hands passed around small strips of paper, each vote a silent testament to the culinary efforts on display. The strips were folded and placed into a cranberry glass bowl, the collective decisions of the group sealed within. Max, taking charge, opened each strip and tallied the scores, his expression shifting as the final count came into view.

"Okay," Max announced, the room falling silent in eager anticipation. "Here it is, everybody. With five votes, the favorite tonight is..." He paused for dramatic effect, pointing to Sterling, who responded with a playful drum roll on the table. Max grinned, "The Salmon en Papillote! Hey, Shug, that's you!"

A round of applause erupted, and Sugar received a congratulatory hug from Max. Jerome helped her into the "Queen Casserole" T-shirt, though Conrad refused to wear the matching "King Casserole" tee, shaking his head with a firm "No!"

Jerome couldn't resist a bit of mischief. "I bet what happened is that the food was too hot, everybody burned their tongue on the first bite, and our taste buds were useless. 'Cause that was not the best dish tonight. I'm sorry," she declared with mock indignation, causing a ripple of laughter and eye-rolls around the table.

Marybelle peacefully interjected, "There's no reason to get so defensive, Jerome."

Leslie chimed in, his voice thoughtful, "The orange flower water was ingenious."

Sugar beamed, "Thank you."

But Burt, still mulling over the dishes, shook his head. "I don't eat salmon, guys. It has gills. I don't do gills."

Jerome handed a slip of paper to Kitty. Kitty's eyes widened as she read it aloud, "Oh. Well, Jerome has written a note: 'The salmon tastes like a spoonful of cunt.' Jerome?!"

A collective gasp went around the room. Marybelle, looking horrified, quickly admonished, "You can't say that. You cannot say that word out loud."

Max, unfazed, leaned back in his chair, a thoughtful look on his face. "You know, there really isn't a word like that for men, is there? Cunt."

Marybelle smacked him, "Maximillian Beedum!"

Max, with a slight grin, continued, "I'm just saying, there isn't really a derogatory term for men that is as ugly as 'cunt.'"

Kitty, slightly embarrassed, muttered, "I apologized for that... Let it go."

Sterling nodded in agreement, "If you think about it, 'Pencil dick' is pretty damn bad."

Conrad pondered this, then shook his head, "'Pencil dick' doesn't have the hard consonant sounds and the abruptness of the word 'cunt.' 'Cunt' is a mighty word."

Marybelle, clearly uncomfortable, put her hands over her ears, "My ears are going to bleed."

Sugar mused, "There's gotta be a bad word for guys. Men deserve a word as horrible as the 'c' word."

Leslie offered, "'Pansy' is the worst, I think."

Conrad nodded, "Jesus, that is awful."

Max continued his analysis. "Yeah, that is a good one, but I think it still lacks the immediate punch and, well, profaneness of 'cunt.' Listen." He leaned forward, as if imparting some great truth. "'You are a pansy!' or 'You are a cunt!' 'Cunt' is so primal."

Marybelle, clearly distressed, looked around the table, "How about, 'You are a FAG!'"

Max's eyes lit up, "She's got it! That's it. The ugly 'ahh' sound followed by the hard 'guh.' FAG. FAG."

Sterling leaned back, the weight of the conversation sinking in. "Phew, that is a loaded word, man. A loaded word."

Leslie, trying to lighten the mood, joked, "If you don't want to say 'Fag' in public, just say 'Flying Above Ground.'"

Sterling chuckled, though the humor was laced with discomfort, "Harsh damn word. Truly harsh."

Florene, always ready with a quip, added, "FAG stands for 'Females Are Gross.'"

Marybelle, clearly reaching her limit, stood up. "Florene!? The whole direction of this conversation hurts. I mean, the men aren't getting any of the derogatory feelings. That's sexist."

Sterling jumped up, animated, "It's the God Damned Truth. F.A.G. is the awfullest. That word is much worse than 'cunt.'"

Sugar shook her head, "Bullshit."

Sterling persisted, "No, it is worse. F.A.G. is meant to question our, uh, masculinity, the very essence of who men are. 'Cunt' just refers to your, your—"

Florene, with a wicked grin, supplied, "Baby funnel."

Burt laughed out loud, breaking the tension slightly.

Kitty, taking Sterling's hand, sighed, "Sometimes, I think men are the stupidest creatures to walk the face of the earth. I really do."

Florene, sensing the need for levity, stood up. "Oh, don't you just love to say bad words? Fuck. Say 'em with me, ladies and gentlemen. Fuck."

The room hesitated, then collectively joined in, "Fuck."

Florene continued, "Shit."

"Shit," echoed the group, except for Marybelle.

"Cocksucker," Florene exclaimed, her voice loud and clear.

The room, now in full swing, shouted back, "Cocksucker!"

Outside, a neighbor walking her dog heard the ruckus and turned away in disgust, quickening her pace as she walked down the sidewalk. The night was still, the air light with the distant hum of the city. Inside, the group dissolved into laughter, the tension of the evening breaking like a fever, leaving them all a little lighter, a little more themselves.

Everyone gradually settled back into their chairs, the earlier intensity giving way to a relaxed camaraderie. The night outside was quiet, the stars twinkling in a cloudless sky, as if to remind them that despite their human dramas, the universe carried on.

Chapter 5

Jerome leaned casually against the counter, a wicked gleam in her eye as she recounted an old story. "And I said, 'Oh yeah, if you had a brain, your balls would fall off, and you'd grow tits.'" Her punchline delivered, she grinned as the room erupted in laughter and applause.

Florene, lounging gracefully, clapped her hands together. "Brilliant. Encore!" she exclaimed, her voice carrying an amused lilt. But Leslie, looking somewhat uncomfortable, turned his attention to the small TV in the corner of the room.

On the screen, a young middle-class couple—the Swinging Singers—stood before a wildly psychedelic kitchen backdrop. The husband held two martini glasses, while the wife filled them from a shaker, her smile wide and bright. "Don't worry that you're no winner," the wife sang sweetly. Together, they chimed, "You can just drink your dinner." As they plopped olives into the glasses and took a sip, both sighed in exaggerated contentment.

Leslie, his discomfort momentarily forgotten, looked up with a sudden burst of enthusiasm. "Cocktails!" he shouted, his voice breaking through the laughter and chatter.

The group moved into the living room, where Leslie

grabbed a bottle of gin from the bar. He moved around the room with a flourish, pouring generous amounts into each glass. *"Vaše zdorov'e!"* he toasted, raising his glass high.

Everyone joined in, raising their glasses and echoing, *"Vaše zdorov'e!"* before taking a collective sip. The air filled with the clink of glasses and the hum of conversation.

Conrad leaned forward with a mischievous glint in his eye. "Well, should we play a game?"

Sterling, already buzzing with excitement, chimed in, "Let's just throw on some tunes and go."

Burt suggested with a grin, "What about we play Agnew's favorite: Pin the Blame on the Donkey?" Laughter rippled through the group, the idea of the game tickling their collective fancy.

Kitty, always eager for a good time, declared, "I want to get inebriated for some reason."

Leslie, sharing her enthusiasm, called out, "Yeah, let's tie one on!" He bounded back to the bar, ready to mix another round of drinks. Kitty whispered something in Sterling's ear, and he nodded with a sly smile.

"Oh, yeah! Hey, has everyone here played 'Railroad Tracks?'" Sterling asked, his voice carrying a note of excitement.

Marybelle, always up for something new, looked to Max. "Oh, what is that? Max, have we played that?"

Jerome, her eyes gleaming, clapped her hands together. "Sterling, I love you. That's the best game." She was practically bouncing with excitement.

Florene interjected with a tale of her own. "When I was thirteen, an albino molested me on the railroad tracks. The moon made his pale skin glow so bright, I just pretended I was having sex with a light bulb." Her tone was casual, as if recounting a mundane event, but her words carried a shock value that made the room pause.

From the bar, Leslie shouted, "Bourbon!" The call was met with a chorus of "yes" from the group, and Leslie dutifully filled their glasses once more.

Sterling, taking charge, explained the rules of "Railroad Tracks." "Now, Railroad Tracks is a physical game. It's about balance and control," he began, his voice taking on a serious tone. Jerome chuckled softly, adding a layer of anticipation. "It's about concentration. The ability to connect your body with your mind. So, Marybelle, you up for it?"

Marybelle nodded enthusiastically. "Hip, hip—" Sterling started, and the room echoed, "Hooray!" Three times they cheered, building up the energy in the room.

As they prepared for the game, the group worked together to clear space. "Just drag that divan back, men," Conrad directed, while Jerome and Kitty moved the coffee table. The middle of the room now open, Leslie grabbed a tiara from the shelf and placed it on Marybelle's head with a flourish.

"Marybelle is the focus. Marybelle is the focus," Leslie declared, his voice filled with mock solemnity.

"What are we going to use? Belts?" Jerome asked, looking around for the necessary props.

Conrad called out to Sugar, "Hey Sugar, run upstairs and grab all my belts from the closet, will you?" Sugar quickly complied, rushing up the stairs and returning with an armful of belts. In her haste, she tripped, crashing into the wall with a soft thud. She paused, wincing at the sharp sting of a rug burn on her knee, before gathering herself and the belts.

Back in the living room, the group arranged the belts in two parallel lines, about shoulder-width apart, creating the "railroad tracks." The belts extended nearly the length of the room, and the game was set.

Sterling explained the rules to Marybelle. "Okay. The idea of this game is that you have to walk on the tracks here we made, and the object is to see if you can walk the entire length of the tracks without falling off. Your feet have to stay on the belts. Get it? The carpet is hot lava."

Marybelle, confident, replied, "But that's so easy."

Jerome grinned, producing a handkerchief. "Yeah, it is. Except you have to walk the railroad tracks while wearing a blindfold." The room erupted in applause as Jerome tied the blindfold over Marybelle's eyes.

"Ready, Marybelle?" Sterling asked, his voice brimming with anticipation.

The group surrounded Marybelle, spinning her from one person to the next, their laughter filling the room. Dizzy and disoriented, Marybelle was finally set at the start of the tracks. She wobbled slightly, arms outstretched, before beginning her tentative walk along the belts.

Meanwhile, Max, Burt, Leslie, and Sterling engaged in a quick game of "Rock, Paper, Scissors" to determine the next player. Burt, victorious with paper over rock, lay down on the ground between the belts, positioning himself directly in Marybelle's path. The group watched, barely containing their laughter.

As Marybelle approached, Florene called out, "Oh, wait, Marybelle. Hold on a second." The room stifled their giggles, the tension palpable. Max made a slicing motion across his neck, signaling for them to stop, but the others held him back, eager to see the prank play out.

"Marybelle, squat down like you're doing a plié," Florene instructed. Marybelle, trusting her friends, did as she was told, squatting low over Burt's face. Burt, unable to resist, began to squirm, his face contorting in exaggerated expressions of ecstasy.

"Marybelle, shake your hips," Kitty encouraged, her voice barely containing her laughter. Marybelle complied, her movements sending the room into fits of barely contained delight.

Conrad, adding to the fun, suggested, "Marybelle, what about some deep knee bends? Up and down and up and down." As Marybelle performed the deep knee bends, Burt's face grew more animated, his exaggerated reactions only fueling the group's amusement.

Finally, Florene called for the big reveal. "Okay, Marybelle, stop. Just one more thing and you win. On the count of three, I want you to take off your blindfold. Ready?"

Marybelle, unaware of the prank, replied, "Uh huh!"

"One... Two... Three!" the group chorused. Marybelle removed the blindfold, blinking as her eyes adjusted to the light. Her back was to the group, her expression one of innocent confusion. She looked down, her gaze slowly traveling from Burt's feet to his face, nestled between her legs.

Through her legs, Burt grinned up at her. "Georgia O'Keefe, M. B. Georgia fucking O'Keefe," he quipped, his voice dripping with humor.

The room exploded with laughter, everyone reveling in the prank's success. Marybelle, her face flushed with embarrassment and frustration, exclaimed, "You are all ASSHOLES! Max?!?" She slapped Max's arm playfully, though her annoyance was evident.

Max, trying to placate her, said, "I tried to stop them."

Marybelle leaned in close, whispering, "It's not funny."

As Burt stood up, wiping his hand with a handkerchief, he chuckled, "I'll remember that for the rest of my life."

Florene, the loudest of them all, let out a hearty laugh. "HA!"

Marybelle, unable to contain her exasperation, stomped her foot. "I could stick my finger in a socket and electrocute myself," she declared dramatically.

Sugar, always quick with a culinary thought, mused, "Good God. I bet it would taste good to deep fry a moonpie."

Jerome, intrigued, leaned closer. "I like the direction you're headed. Keep talking."

Kitty, her eyes widening at the thought, leaned in as well. "Dear me, that sounds delicious."

Sugar, lost in her culinary fantasy, continued, "Well, you could lightly batter two moonpies and deep fry them until they're golden. Then you drain those and spread softened vanilla ice cream between the moonpies and then dip that whole thing into chocolate. And then you freeze it.

"I think I'm in love with you," Jerome batted her false eyelashes.

Kitty swooned, "Dear me, that sounds delicious."

Chapter 6

Florene, with a mischievous grin, pulled a small tin container from her purse. The air buzzed with curiosity as she held it up. "I have another game for us to play," she announced, her eyes glinting with a tease. "Max, come to mama."

Burt, sensing what was coming, looked on anxiously, his body tense with anticipation. Max, always up for a bit of fun, approached with a curious smile. "What kind of game?" he asked, his voice tinged with intrigue.

Jerome, leaning in to get a better look, asked, "Is that a recipe tin?"

Florene whispered under her breath, "A special kind," her tone laced with suggestive mystery.

Marybelle, always eager for novelty, leaned in closer, her eyes wide with excitement. "What are the recipes?" she asked, her voice tinged with innocent curiosity.

Florene lifted the tin, revealing its contents to the group. Marybelle's eyes lit up at the sight of the tin's decoration. "Look, it has cute little apples on it," she exclaimed, her voice filled with delight.

Sterling, less interested in the aesthetics and more in the substance, interjected, "Screw the apples, what's inside?" He grabbed the box from Florene and opened it, revealing recipe cards neatly divided by tabs: Appetizers, Salads, Entrees, and Dessert.

Sterling, perplexed, flipped through the cards. "Recipes?" he asked, confusion etched on his face.

Kitty, peering over his shoulder, raised an eyebrow. "What did you expect to find in a recipe box?"

Florene, taking a sip of her gin, smirked. "Well, they're special recipes," she teased, her tone hinting at the unconventional nature of the contents.

Leslie, ever the joker, added, "Is my brain shrinking? Can you tell if your brain is shrinking?" His offhand comment drew a few chuckles from the group, lightening the mood.

Marybelle, now holding an appetizer recipe card, examined it closely. The card had tiny apples in the corner, adding to its quaint charm. "It just has a list of ingredients," she said, puzzled. "Ice? I don't understand. Put an ice cube in your—" She gasped, flipping the card around to reveal a pin-up of a naked woman on the reverse side. Her cheeks flushed as she realized what they were all staring at.

Florene couldn't contain her laughter any longer, bursting out with a hearty laugh that echoed through the room.

The group moved to the poolside, the warm night air wrapping around them like a comforting blanket. They settled into their chairs, martinis in hand, and cigarettes glowing in the dark. Leslie mused aloud, "The funny thing is, I've fantasized about burying my own shrink."

Sterling, leaning back with a mischievous grin, quipped, "I fantasize a lot about burying things."

Jerome, her face a mask of mock concern, responded, "The implications of that statement disturb me."

Florene shared her own bizarre fantasy. "I have this recurring fantasy that my mother lives in my flower garden, buried up to the neck. And she knits flies' wings into oven mitts with her tongue. And when the summer's over, I dig mother up and carve out her insides to make a jack o'lantern for the front porch."

Sugar, looking bewildered, simply said, "That's weird."

Florene, with a deadpan expression, replied, "My mother?"

Kitty chimed in, sharing her own odd experience. "The weirdest thing for me was at the grocery store one day. I was picking up a container of Quaker oats, and the Quaker on the front winked at me."

Max, shaking his head, dismissed her story. "Not fantasy. Delusion."

Jerome was eager to explore the strange contents of the recipe tin and called out, "I want to look at that recipe box again. Who has it?" Sterling handed it to her, and Jerome pulled out another card, her curiosity piqued.

Max, leaning back with a grin, declared, "I dream about cars, hamburgers, and my wife's ass." Marybelle playfully smacked his arm, chiding him, "You're so macho."

Jerome, reading aloud from the card, said, "Listen to this, people. This is crazy. 'Here's a special recipe. A recipe of ME. 1 cup true devotion...'"

Kitty, rolling her eyes, muttered, "I know where this is going."

Jerome continued, "'A tablespoon of harlot.'"

Marybelle, intrigued, asked, "What's 'harlot' for a man?"

Conrad, with a sly grin, answered, "Normal."

Burt, joining in the fun, shouted, "I'm a harlot. I'm a harlot." The group laughed, enjoying the playful banter.

Jerome, shushing them, pressed on. "Shh, shhh. Okay. 'Two hands full of love.' Oh, Jesus Christ. And here, the clincher. 'As much time as you can spare.' Awwwww."

Sterling, clearly confused, asked, "What kind of recipe is that? Am I missing something?"

Leslie, with a sudden revelation, exclaimed, "Holy shit. I just thought of something. 'Casserole' has the word ASS in it."

The room fell silent for a moment before bursting into laughter, the absurdity of the statement hitting them all at once.

Burt, feeling the effects of the night, confessed, "Forgive me, people, but I've got to be honest right now. I am capital 'H'... horny!"

Florene, with a knowing look, retorted, "That is not news."

Sugar, chiming in, added, "I was going to say that too."

Leslie remarked, "I don't say 'horny' because it reminds me of zebras."

Conrad, puzzled, replied, "Zebras don't have horns."

Leslie, undeterred, continued, "But they should."

Florene, eager to keep the game going, urged, "Jerome, read another one."

Jerome, flipping through the cards, found another gem. "Oh my, it all gets worse. Get your waders on, boys. All it says on this one is 'Turn to the person on your left and tell them one thing you like about them.' And in parentheses, it says 'physical.'"

Leslie, seizing the opportunity, turned to Sugar.

"Sugar, I think you have a beautiful mouth. You have lips like landing strips. And I should know because I want to land there."

The group groaned in mock disapproval. "Boo!" they chorused, but the laughter in their eyes betrayed their amusement.

Jerome, shaking her head, declared, "No, no, no. We are not going to do this."

Florene insisted, "Oh, just do it quick. Start with Sugar and just turn and blurt out whatever it is you want to say and then right on to the next."

Kitty, always game for a bit of fun, agreed. "Perfect!"

Jerome, with a resigned sigh, said, "Oh shit."

Sugar, taking a deep breath, prepared to begin. "Ready? I'm going to turn my head... Now." She turned to Max on her left. "Max, you are gorgeous and every woman sitting here thinks so too."

Kitty, playfully scolding, said, "Sugar!" She reached over and pinched Sugar, eliciting a giggle.

Marybelle, her voice tinged with mock indignation, added, "He's my husband!"

Jerome, jumping in, confessed, "I'll admit it. Max is the kind of man you want to climb."

Conrad, keeping the game moving, reminded them, "I thought we were going to say it and move on."

Sugar, with a teasing smile, said, "Don't be jealous."

Max turned to Conrad. "Conny, you're pretty too."

Jerome, eager to keep the momentum, urged, "Max, go...."

Max, slightly flustered, turned to Kitty. "Kitty, you have great tits."

Kitty, with a mock demure smile, replied, "Why, thank you."

Sterling, laughing, chimed in, "I'm with you all the way, buddy."

Jerome, keeping things moving, directed, "Kitty, your left. Move, move."

Kitty, playfully exasperated, responded, "I'm going, bossy." She turned to Conrad. "Conny, your eyes, I seriously cannot look you in the eyes for too long because if I do, I just want to jump on you and take you on a Kitty Vacation."

Sterling, grinning, said, "Down, Kitty, down." Kitty, laughing, purred and pawed at Conrad like a playful kitten.

Conrad, taking his turn, looked to Marybelle. "Marybelle."

Max, feigning protectiveness, warned, "Watch it now."

Conrad, with a grin, continued, "Marybelle. To put it simply, I love your ass. I love every curve and slope of your buttocks. I love to spend time with you, but watching you walk away is one of the supreme pleasures of my life. If I could, I would eat every meal off your ass. I want to make a mold of your ass so I can hang it on the wall next to my bed and fall asleep each night staring at your ass," he said, his tone teasing but earnest. The room erupted in laughter, the absurdity of the statement breaking the tension.

Sugar, her expression a mix of amusement and mild annoyance, interjected, "Conrad, really?" Her tone hinted at a warning, but there was a twinkle in her eye that suggested she wasn't entirely serious.

Conrad, sensing he might have gone too far, added quickly, "Now, Sugar, don't be jealous."

Marybelle, caught off guard and visibly flustered,

struggled to find her words. "Um, uh..." She turned to Sterling, desperate to shift the focus. "You have strong-looking hands," she stammered, trying to regain her composure.

Sterling, slightly bemused, accepted the compliment with a casual, "Thanks. I think." He then turned his attention to Florene, who was watching him intently. "Florene..." he began, his voice trailing off as she leaned in closer, her perfume enveloping him.

"You... uh... you give me goose pimples. And you smell really nice," Sterling finished, his voice almost a whisper, caught in the intoxicating allure of her presence.

Florene smiled, her voice silky smooth. "Estee Lauder," she purred, before turning to Burt. "Oh, you already know, Smooches," she said, leaning in for a passionate kiss. The room watched, half-amused, half-envious.

Sterling, feeling slightly cheated, quipped, "Not fair, they're married."

Burt, with a smile, turned to Leslie. "Leslie. You are a beautiful guy inside and out, and I'm glad to call you my friend."

The room erupted in a chorus of "Awwwwww," the sincerity of Burt's words touching everyone.

Burt, with a playful glint in his eye, added, "I'm kidding. Actually, I've always admired your eyebrows."

Jerome, taking stock of the room, asked, "Is that it? Did we finally make it around?"

Leslie, genuinely touched, responded, "I'm moved, Burt. Really, I'm stirred."

Jerome, eager to move on, urged, "Next one, next one. Let's get this over."

Sugar, sensing the group's waning enthusiasm, suggested, "We don't have to keep going."

But Conrad, always the instigator, insisted, "Yes, now we do. We can't stop in the middle."

Kitty, still puzzled by the rules, asked, "What kind of a game is this? How do we know who's winning and who's losing?"

Max, shrugging, answered, "Not a clue."

Jerome, with a glint of excitement, exclaimed, "Shush, shush. I love this one. I do. 'Lay on the ground with your heads touching and let your brains synchronize.'"

The couples lay on the ground by the pool, forming a circle with their heads touching. The night sky stretched above them, the stars twinkling like sapphires. Silence covered the group, a gentle breeze rustling the palm trees. The cool desert air provided a stark contrast to the warmth of the day.

They lay there, unsure of what to expect, the silence only broken by the occasional giggle or whispered comment. They made the sound of electricity, "zzzzzzzz," and laughed, their voices carrying into the night. Their heads close together, they felt a strange, almost mystical connection, as if their thoughts and emotions were merging in the stillness of the desert night.

After a few minutes, Sterling broke the silence, his voice tinged with amusement. "Maybe we should just try another one," he suggested, his tone light and playful.

The group, grateful for the suggestion, agreed in unison, "Yeah. That's a good idea." They slowly sat up, the magic of the moment lingering in the air as they looked at each other, smiles playing on their lips. The game might have been silly, but it had brought them closer, creating a bond that would last long after the night was over.

The air was thick with the sweet scent of desert blooms and the warm, soothing sounds of night insects. Florene, with a mischievous glint in her eye, picked up the recipe tin once more and pulled out another card. She held it up, capturing everyone's attention.

"You all ready?" she asked, her voice playful. Burt looked particularly anxious, perhaps sensing the mischief in the air.

Leslie asked, "Angel, flask?"

Jerome, chuckling, handed him a sleek silver flask. He took a hearty swig before passing it back, and Jerome followed suit, shivering at the potent taste. "Mercy," she exclaimed, the warmth of the liquor spreading through her.

Sterling, noticeably tipsy, leaned over Florene's shoulder, eager to see the next game. "The card says, 'Grab each other and start swinging,'" he read aloud.

"Swinging? How do we do that?" Kitty asked, puzzled.

"Go to the park?" Marybelle suggested innocently, eliciting a few chuckles.

Sterling, clearly inspired, had a different idea. "Oh, I know! I know. I think if two people get like this—Conny, come here a sec." Sterling and Conny locked arms, demonstrating the concept. "Then, Kitty, come here. Sit on our arms. Then we can swing back and forth like this."

Kitty, giggling, agreed, "Oh, it's fun. We did this when we were kids."

Jerome, always up for a bit of fun, quickly jumped in.

"I want to try that. Leslie, you and Burt swing me." The men linked arms, and Jerome sat, swinging with a carefree joy that felt almost childlike. "I've never done this before. It's so freeing," she declared, laughing.

Not wanting to miss out, Marybelle chimed in, "I want a turn!" The group was in high spirits, laughter echoing under the starlit sky.

Suddenly, there was a small mishap. Kitty, caught up in the moment, accidentally fell from Sterling and Conrad's arms. As she did, her dress slipped, revealing her very sizable tits. "Oh, jeepers!" she exclaimed, a mix of embarrassment and amusement.

The group stopped, momentarily taken aback. Conrad, unable to help himself, blurted out, "Holy mother of gifts."

Sterling, laughing, added, "That's my gal..."

Burt simply said, "Wow."

Jerome teased, "Kitty, I feel a little less than..."

Kitty, undeterred and clearly embracing the evening's wild energy, announced, "Mama wants to swim." With a boldness that surprised even herself, she stripped off the rest of her clothing and confidently walked into the pool, the cool water welcoming her.

"Catch me, catch me!" she called, her laughter infectious.

Not to be outdone, Burt followed suit, shedding his clothes to reveal a very meaty dick, and leaped into the pool.

Florene, with a carefree shrug, joined in, stumbling toward Conrad as she unzipped the back of her dress. "Come on in, boys. What are you waiting for?" she beckoned, letting her dress fall to the ground.

Conrad quickly stripped down and dove in.

Marybelle, feeling a mix of excitement and hesitation, stripped to her bra and panties before joining them. "Let's play Marco Polo!" she suggested, her voice filled with excitement.

Conrad gave her a playful smack on the backside as she entered the water. "You do have a great ass," he commented, his tone appreciative.

Marybelle, blushing fiercely, stammered, "Oh, Conny, I, um, thanks." As he moved past her, stepping up onto a pool step, she caught a glimpse of his heavy hanging manhood and her eyes widened. She felt a wave of dizziness and swooned slightly, only to be caught in Conrad's arms as the water splashed around them.

The group, now fully immersed in the spontaneous pool party, splashed and played, their laughter mingling with the gentle lapping of the water. The night air was filled with joy and a sense of carefree abandon, each of them basking in the moment's freedom and exhilaration. As they played, and kissed, and laughed, and groped, the bonds of their friendships deepened.

In the kitchen, Sugar carefully arranged a display of Jello salads on the counter. Each salad was a vibrant hue, beaming under the soft kitchen lights in a riot of bright reds, neon greens, yellows, and oranges. The salads seemed almost too beautiful to eat, their translucent surfaces shimmering like jewels.

As Sugar admired her handiwork, she took a sip of her vodka, feeling the smooth burn of the alcohol warming her. Just then, she heard a voice behind her.

"Is that Jello salad?" Max's voice was a blend of surprise and delight. Sugar turned, her breath catching at the sight of him. God, he was sexy. His eyes sparkled with genuine excitement, making her heart skip a beat.

"I love Jello salad," he continued, stepping closer. His presence filled the room, making everything else seem to fade into the background.

Sugar smiled, a bit dazed by the mix of alcohol and the electricity in the air. "I like it too," she murmured, her voice softer than usual. "Look how it glistens in the light." She gestured to the salads, but her eyes never left Max's.

Max reached out, his fingers hovering over the gelatinous surface. "A handful of Jello would feel so good," he mused, his tone suggestive. Sugar, feeling a flush rise to her cheeks, handed him a serving spoon, her fingers brushing against his.

Max grinned, digging his fingers into the Jello and scooping out a generous portion. He brought it to his mouth, savoring the texture and taste. "Mmmmmmm," he hummed in approval. Then, with a mischievous glint in his eye, he scooped up another handful and offered it to Sugar.

She hesitated only for a moment before leaning in, allowing him to feed her. The cool, sweet dessert was a stark contrast to the warmth spreading through her body. A bit of Jello clung to her chin, and before she could wipe it away, Max leaned in, his lips brushing against her skin as he licked it off. The gesture sent a jolt through her, and suddenly they were kissing, feverishly, passionately.

Outside by the pool, the scene had taken on a life of its own. The group, already buzzing with the thrill of the evening and the effects of alcohol, had shed their inhibitions along with their clothes. They became a tangle of wet, naked bodies, moving together in a primal dance of desire. The water lapped at the sides of the pool.

Conrad, lost in the moment, was thrusting his raging hard on deep into Marybelle, who, in her drunken state, flopped around in his arms half unconscious. Nearby, Jerome, Burt, and Kitty were tangled in a knot of limbs, their laughter mingling with moans of pleasure. Florene moved between Leslie and Sterling, fondling their naked wet bodies, sending shivers through both men.

Back in the kitchen, Max lifted Sugar onto the counter, pushing aside the Jello salads in their frenzy. Her dress hiked up, slid off her panties and entered her. His pants fell quickly to the floor as she wrapped her legs around his waist. With each thrust, they moved against each other, their grunts and moans filling the kitchen. The Jello, once a beautiful centerpiece, now became a sticky, colorful mess as they rolled in it.

By the pool, the chaos continued. Burt, eyeing Conrad's conquest, called out, "I want a taste of that one!" Conrad, without hesitation, slid away from the barely conscious Marybelle, who was quickly claimed by Burt. As Conrad moved towards the edge of the pool, Florene appeared, pulling him into a deep kiss.

Kitty and Jerome, lost in their own world, playfully fondled each other's breasts, giggling like schoolgirls. The pool water, now a whirl of movement and light, reflected the electric energy of the air. The group, now a single, writhing mass of pleasure and abandon, was lost in the moment, their grunts and moans echoing into the quiet desert night. The stars above seemed to dance in time with the rhythm of their bodies, the universe itself pulsated, shooting streams of thick milky pleasure into the night.

Chapter 7

As the dawn light began to bathe the scene in a soft glow, the aftermath of the previous night became visible. The once pristine poolside area was now a messy tableau of discarded clothes and intertwined bodies. Naked limbs lay askew, and the occasional groan of awakening drifted through the air, breaking the stillness of the early morning.

Marybelle stirred first, the realization of her surroundings dawning slowly. She groaned and sat up abruptly, clutching at the rumpled dress barely covering her. Her eyes widened in horror as she took in the disheveled state of her friends, sprawled around the pool like fallen revelers. A gasp escaped her lips, loud enough to rouse the others from their stupor.

The guests scrambled to cover themselves, hastily grabbing at clothing and casting embarrassed glances at one another. The night's indulgence seemed distant now, replaced by a palpable discomfort and a rush to depart. Marybelle, her face flushed with shame, gathered her belongings and hurriedly dressed, her movements quick and jerky.

Burt and Florene, however, seemed immune to the collective embarrassment. They exchanged knowing glances and, with a casual air, took each other's hands. Laughing softly, they sauntered toward the gate, their naked forms unabashed, carrying their clothes with an ease that suggested a lack of regret. Their departure, hand in hand, was almost serene amidst the scattered remnants of the night.

As the others hurried away, front doors slammed shut in quick succession, the sound echoing through the quiet neighborhood. The last vestiges of the party were swept away, leaving behind only the stillness of the early morning.

Sugar awoke alone in her bed, her head pounding. She reached for a glass of water, sipping slowly as she tried to piece together the events. The sound of the shower running in the adjoining bathroom brought a flicker of hope. She glanced toward the door, listening as the water stopped and Conrad emerged, a towel slung low around his waist.

He moved with a deliberate calm, drying off and dressing without so much as a glance in her direction. Sugar watched him, a knot of unease forming in her stomach. "What time is it?" she asked, her voice thick and uncertain.

Conrad didn't respond, continuing to dress with an air of detached efficiency.

"What's going on? Where are you going?" she pressed, her voice tinged with confusion and a hint of desperation.

Conrad finally looked at her, his expression unreadable. "The Country Club," he replied tersely, his tone flat.

As he continued to gather his belongings, Sugar sat

up, trying to bridge the distance between them. "Why don't you get back in bed? I wanna show you something," she offered, attempting a playful smile.

Conrad paused, his gaze cold and distant. "I've seen it already," he said, his words cutting through the room like a knife.

He turned and left, the door closing with a finality that echoed in the quiet room. Sugar sat in stunned silence, the sting of rejection sharp and painful. She glanced down at her knee, noticing a sticky residue from the night before. Mechanically, she opened a drawer and applied a band-aid, the small action a futile attempt to cover a deeper wound. The morning light filtered in, casting long shadows across the room, as Sugar sat in quiet contemplation of the night that had permanently changed everything.

Chapter 8

Kitty stood in her kitchen, her hands deftly working on mixing up a cake batter. The rhythmic sound of her stirring filled the room, but the silence was palpable. Sterling entered quietly, pausing at the sight of her. He stood there, watching her work, unsure of what to say or do. Kitty glanced up, a big, artificial smile plastered on her face, trying to maintain a facade of normalcy.

"I squeezed some orange juice for you," she offered, nodding towards the table where a glass sat waiting.

Sterling picked up the glass and took a sip, the cold liquid offering little comfort. The silence stretched, awkward and thick with unspoken tension.

"I'm going to the Country Club for a game with Leslie and Conny," Sterling finally said, his voice sounding almost apologetic.

"Okay," Kitty replied, sifting flour into the bowl. "Will you be back for supper?"

Sterling hesitated, the weight of the previous night's events hanging heavily in the air. "I'm not sure. Depends on—"

Kitty cut him off with a bright, forced cheerfulness. "Well, just take your time then."

The room felt stifling, the tension palpable. Sterling

watched her for a moment longer, searching for something, anything, that might bridge the growing chasm between them.

"Would you like me to make anything in particular?" Kitty asked, her voice betraying no hint of the turmoil she felt inside.

"Whatever you'd like to eat," Sterling responded, his discomfort evident.

Kitty's smile remained fixed, a mask hiding her true feelings. "Okay. I'll try the chicken. Maybe I'll try Marybelle's recipe. You seemed to like it."

Sterling shifted awkwardly, nodding. "Sure, if it isn't too much trouble."

"No trouble at all," Kitty assured him, her voice light and breezy. She smiled again, a strained, plastic smile that didn't reach her eyes. Sterling mirrored her smile, then turned and left the room, the door closing with a soft click.

As soon as he was gone, Kitty's smile faded. She reached for the bottle of red food coloring and squeezed a few drops into the batter. Her movements became frantic, the mixer whirring loudly as she blended the red dye into the cake mix, her expression taut with barely contained emotion.

Meanwhile, outside, Sterling walked briskly down the driveway, glancing furtively up and down the street to make sure no one saw him. The previous night's indiscretions weighed heavily on him, filling him with a deep sense of shame. Just as he reached the end of the driveway, Conrad pulled up in his car and honked the horn, the sound jarring and out of place in the quiet morning.

Sterling cringed, mortified by the noise. Conrad,

however, seemed unbothered, laughing as Sterling climbed into the car.

"We don't need to play a round if you don't really want to," Sterling suggested, his voice hesitant.

"Golf relaxes me," Conrad replied, a grin spreading across his face as he pulled away from the curb.

They drove in silence for a few moments, the atmosphere in the car heavy with unspoken tension. When they arrived at Leslie's house, Conrad honked again, and Leslie came out, joining them with a cheerful greeting.

"Howdy, friends," Leslie said, settling into the back seat.

The drive continued in silence until they passed a woman walking on the sidewalk, her figure perfectly proportioned, a scarf and sunglasses completing her chic look. Conrad let out a low whistle.

"Jesus, would you look at that bitch. Man, what a rack. You've got it lucky, Sterling," Conrad said, glancing sideways at Sterling.

"Lucky?" Sterling echoed, his voice uncertain.

"Sure, you got a wife with great tits who lets you do whatever you want. Sounds like heaven to me," Conrad continued, chuckling. "Poor ole Les has a wife built like a man, and I'm tied up with a cadaver. I can't help it if I get horny. You know, I'm a guy. Our job is to be horny." He laughed again, punching Sterling playfully on the shoulder.

"Right?" Conrad looked in the rearview mirror, catching Leslie's eye.

"Right, Les?" he prompted.

Leslie hesitated, then replied, "I'll get back to you on that."

Conrad shrugged, his laughter ringing out in the confined space of the car. "Yeah, it's no big deal. No big deal," he muttered, almost as if trying to convince himself. The car sped along, the morning sun casting long shadows as they headed toward the Country Club, leaving behind the tangled emotions and unfinished conversations of the night before.

In her dressing area, Sugar carefully peeled off the old band-aid, wincing slightly as she examined the gross scab on her knee. She quickly replaced it with a fresh band-aid, then moved towards the phone, her fingers hesitating over the dial. Taking a deep breath, she dialed a number, then quickly hung up, feeling unsure.

After a moment of pacing, she picked up the phone again and dialed. The line connected, and Max's voice came through.

"Hello?" Max's voice was calm, yet cautious.

"Max, thank god it's you. It's Sugar. I'm so sorry about—" Sugar began, her voice tinged with anxiety.

Max cut her off with a quiet, reassuring tone, clearly trying to keep the conversation discreet. "Don't worry. You were a tigress last night."

Suddenly, another voice joined the line. "Hello?" Marybelle's voice was clear, causing Max to shift his tone abruptly.

"I got it," he said quickly, his voice masking any previous familiarity.

Sugar panicked for a moment, the unexpected turn catching her off guard. "Marybelle. Hi Marybelle. I was just calling to—"

Marybelle sounded puzzled. "Sugar?"

Max, sensing the tension, quickly excused himself.

"I'll let you two gals talk." The line clicked, and he was gone, leaving Sugar fumbling for words.

"What is it, Sugar?" Marybelle asked, her tone genuinely curious.

Sugar quickly composed herself, trying to sound casual. "I just wanted you to know that I washed and dried your casserole dish."

There was a brief pause, as Marybelle processed the seemingly mundane reason for the call. "Oh. Well, thank you...um..."

Sugar felt the awkwardness of the moment pressing down on her. "Okay, I gotta run," she blurted out, hanging up the phone with a shaky hand.

Marybelle stared at the phone, a look of confusion and suspicion spreading across her face. The line between the casual exchange and the underlying tension was palpable, leaving her with an uneasy feeling.

Chapter 9

As night descended upon the desert, the sky transformed into a canvas of deep, velvety blues and intoxicating purples, reminiscent of a luxurious tapestry. The silhouettes of distant mountains became mysterious, shadowy outlines against the twilight, exuding a sense of enigmatic allure. The air cooled, carrying with it the seductive whispers of desert winds that caressed the arid terrain like a lover's breath. The serene quiet of the desert evening was punctuated by the occasional rustle of nocturnal creatures awakening, adding an undercurrent of anticipation to the stillness.

Inside the Bainbridge estate, Conrad prepared himself with an air of ritualistic precision. He donned a terry cloth men's shower skirt and entered his bathroom, locking the door behind him. His movements were methodical, almost mechanical, reflecting a tightly held anxiety that permeated his demeanor. He set up a TV tray next to the toilet, carefully arranging a flask of scotch, a bottle of pills, a small hand mirror, a silver Gillette razor, and a grooming set.

Conrad closed the toilet lid and sat down, positioning the tray with an almost reverent precision. He took a pill from the bottle, swallowing it with a swig from the flask.

The lid clicked back into place as he set the flask down, each movement deliberate and controlled, a stark contrast to the storm brewing within him.

Opening the grooming set, Conrad laid out its contents with the precision of a surgeon preparing for a delicate operation. He picked up a small pair of tweezers and the mirror, meticulously plucking stray nose hairs and the tiny black hairs along his ears. Each tool was carefully cleaned and replaced in its designated spot, the ritual serving as a temporary balm to his inner turmoil.

He then moved on to his mustache, trimming and combing it with a small mustache comb, ensuring each hair was perfectly in place. Satisfied with his appearance, Conrad took another drink from the flask and swallowed a second pill.

With a quiet sigh, he untwisted the razor, removed the blade, and set it aside. Leaning back against the toilet tank, he spread his legs. In a practiced motion, he made a quick cut on his inner thigh, the sharp sting followed by the sight of blood beading up on his skin. The sight seemed to bring him a measure of calm, a release from the tension coiled within him.

Conrad made another cut, then another, each one adding to the thin, threadlike scars already decorating his thigh. He watched the blood drip slowly, almost mesmerized by the process. As the crimson droplets splattered against the pale tiles, he took another drink, the alcohol dulling the edges of his thoughts.

In the quiet of the bathroom, with only the sound of his breathing and the faint drip of blood, Conrad found a moment of peace, however fleeting. The ritual, as unsettling as it was, offered him a strange comfort, a way to manage life. The bathroom light cast harsh shadows, highlighting the stark reality of his actions, yet in this private space, he could confront his demons tomorrow.

At Kitty and Sterling's house, the air was thick with a tension that neither spoke of. Kitty approached the door of Sterling's den, hesitating before knocking gently. Sterling sat inside, seemingly engrossed in his book, the room cloaked in an awkward silence. Kitty's voice broke the stillness, soft but clear.

"Well, I'm going up to bed," she announced, her tone carrying an undercurrent of unspoken questions.

Sterling glanced up briefly, his expression unreadable. "I'll be up in a bit," he responded, his eyes quickly returning to the pages before him. Kitty lingered for a moment longer, her presence a silent inquiry, before turning and leaving the room.

As soon as she was gone, Sterling's demeanor changed. He checked to make sure Kitty was truly out of sight, then discreetly pulled out a small magazine that he had hidden within the larger book. His movements were quick and practiced, a secret ritual he had clearly performed many times before. The cover of the magazine was hidden from view, its contents known only to Sterling. He glanced around once more, ensuring his solitude, before slipping his hand into his fly, the room once again silent, save for the soft rustle of his hand moving up and down inside his pants.

Down the block in Florene and Burt's lavish estate, the evening was filled with a sense of indulgence and ease. Florene lounged in a bubble bath, the champagne in her glass sparkling under the soft light. The pink marble of the tub complemented her relaxed demeanor as Burt, clad in a bathrobe, sat on the edge, carefully shaving her legs. His voice carried a playful note as he spoke.

"I'm warning you right now, I'm having this drumstick for dinner tonight," Burt teased, playfully biting her leg.

Florene responded with a contented murmur, "Mmmm. We should really do that more often."

Burt chuckled, shaking his head slightly. "I can't believe how uptight our friends are. It's never taken that long to get a group in the mood before."

Florene grinned, her eyes glinting with amusement. "Oh, they're just a bunch of Catholics," she quipped.

"Worse," Burt countered with a mock serious tone.

"Vegetarians?" Florene suggested, causing them both to burst into laughter.

Burt's laughter was warm as he replied, "And that's why I married you."

With a playful flick of her wrist, Florene gestured towards her glass. "Mama needs more champie."

Burt obliged, pouring more champagne into her glass. As the bubbles settled, Florene casually remarked, "That Kitty Bloom sure has nice tits."

Burt moved closer, a mischievous glint in his eye. "So do you, pussycat," he said, leaning down to kiss her breast. Florene laughed, enjoying the moment.

"You're a little rascal, you know that?" she teased.

Burt smiled, a gleam of curiosity in his eyes. "So what was Kitty's husband like?"

Florene shrugged, a hint of disappointment in her voice. "Nothing to write home about. Nice guy. But he just didn't seem to be into it."

Burt looked genuinely surprised. "Not into you? Guy musta been crocked beyond repair."

Florene shook her head, still incredulous. "But that Conny, on the other hand. Did you see his—"

"Oh, I saw it," Burt interrupted, grinning. "Unfuckingbelievable."

As Burt finished shaving her legs, he rinsed them off with the handheld shower, the water cascading over the marble. The scene was intimate, comfortable, a glimpse into their private world.

"What are we having for dinner? I'm getting hungry," Burt asked, his tone casual.

Florene smiled, leaning back in the tub. "I made your favorite."

"Ham and green beans?" Burt guessed, his eyes lighting up.

"Green bean Florene," she corrected, downing her champagne.

Burt cheered, "Yee-haw! Fly me to the moon!"

Florene laughed, shaking her head. "Oh, not the backdoor tonight, baby. Mama's not up for that."

Burt whined playfully, then burst into a teasing song, "If you suck my peter, this guy won't be no cheater, 'cause baby I'm about respect."

Florene laughed heartily, her eyes sparkling with affection. "Jesus, I love you. Bring it here!"

Burt opened his robe wide, like a bird spreading its wings, and Florene's laughter echoed around the bathroom, a sound of pure joy and contentment.

Chapter 10

In the quiet of the neighborhood, the majestic mountains stood tall and silent, casting long shadows over the homes below. The scene was still, almost as if the world held its breath. From behind their doors, Kitty, Florene, Marybelle, and Jerome cautiously stepped out, each glancing around nervously as they made their way toward Sugar's house. The air between them was thick with unspoken tension, their steps echoing in the stillness.

Inside Sugar's kitchen, the atmosphere was equally strained. The casseroles, neatly lined up on the counter, seemed to stand as silent witnesses to the unease among the women. Sugar tried to break the ice, her voice overly cheerful.

"This looks delicious, Kitty. What is it?" she asked, trying to sound enthusiastic.

Kitty forced a smile, her voice lacking its usual confidence. "I made my famous Pigs on a Cloud."

The others looked on with varying degrees of confusion and discomfort as they eyed the Pyrex dish. It was an odd concoction of little smokies standing upright in a fluffy, white mixture that defied identification. Jerome stared at it, bewildered, while the room fell into an uncomfortable silence.

"So, are we supposed to use the little wiener as a utensil?" Sugar joked, trying to lighten the mood.

Jerome's blunt response cut through the awkwardness. "Jesus, the tension in here is as thick as Nixon."

Florene nodded in agreement, and Marybelle sighed, her voice tinged with frustration. "We don't need to talk about it."

But Jerome wasn't having it. "It's ridiculous, we can't even look each other in the eye. C'mon, it was just sex."

Marybelle shook her head, looking down. "I'm not a sex person."

Florene suggested, "What we need to do is get everybody back together again for another casserole party. Just move on."

Kitty looked horrified at the suggestion. "Are you insane?"

"I don't know," Marybelle murmured, uncertainty creeping into her voice.

Jerome laid it out plainly. "Either that, or we all turn into bitter, dried-up old prunes..."

Marybelle looked up, her expression troubled. "What we did was not normal."

Jerome shrugged. "What we did was get bombed."

A silence settled over them, heavy with the weight of their actions. Sugar finally spoke, her voice soft. "Jerome's right. We just got a little too drunk, is all."

Florene snorted. "Right - blame the liquor!"

Jerome, undeterred, pressed on. "And you know that anything that happens when you're drunk doesn't count."

Kitty shook her head, her voice tinged with regret.

"We were much better off before we made it a contest."

Marybelle sighed deeply. "I don't know, we just trampled all over our vows."

Jerome's patience was running thin. "Grow up! We're animals, get used to it. There will be no more dissenting voices. We're a club, and we stick together no matter what."

Florene, sensing the need for a gesture of unity, stepped forward. "C'mon. What would Gloria Steinem do? Group hug!!!"

Reluctantly, they all moved closer, forming a slightly uncomfortable circle. Florene grinned, "We could burn our bras, would that make you feel better?"

The women exchanged glances, some smiling, others still looking uncertain. The awkwardness lingered, but the shared moment seemed to hold a promise of moving forward, however tentative.

Chapter 11

The atmosphere in the room was tense, thick with unspoken words and lingering glances. Everyone sipped their cocktails and smoked in near silence, the quiet punctuated only by the occasional cough or nervous laugh. The air seemed charged with an electric quality, as if any moment it might crackle and spark.

Sterling cleared his throat, trying to break the uncomfortable silence. "What, uh... dishes are we going to be voting on tonight?" he asked, his voice hesitant.

Sugar, attempting to keep things light, began listing the dishes with forced cheerfulness. "Well... We have Kitty's Pigs on a Cloud..."

As she spoke, Conrad's eyes wandered, fixating on Kitty's breasts. She caught him staring, and he quickly cleared his throat, turning away in the opposite direction.

"And Marybelle's Cheesy Italian..." Sugar continued, her voice faltering slightly.

Max took a sip of his martini, offering Sugar a knowing wink. She smiled nervously, feeling the weight of the unspoken tension in the room.

Sugar listed the final dish. "Uh... Jerome's Chicken Enchilada..."

Leslie, trying to lighten the mood, chimed in, "Oh, I

love your Chicken Enchilada."

Jerome stood up and made her way to the bar, her movements purposeful as if to avoid any eye contact.

Sugar hesitated, then asked, "Florene... I can't remember. What did you make?"

Florene casually set out a dish of mysterious-looking cookies on the coffee table. "I didn't make a casserole," she said with a sly smile.

Marybelle looked confused. "But you said...?"

Florene waved off the concern, smiling mischievously. "I made an appetizer."

Marybelle, already nibbling on a cookie, exclaimed, "They're delicious!"

Kitty, her mood lightening, added, "Cookies as an appetizer. I love you."

Florene grinned, enjoying the intrigue. "I call them Identity Bars."

"Identity Bars?" Sugar echoed, raising an eyebrow.

"Oui," Florene confirmed, a twinkle in her eye.

Burt leaned in close to Florene and whispered, "Just like the magazine." Florene stifled a laugh, nodding slightly.

Sterling, munching on a cookie, remarked, "Is it a bar, is it a cookie, is it a cake?"

"Lord, yummy, yummy," Kitty chimed in, savoring the treat.

Conrad, unable to resist, leaned towards Florene and murmured, "Mmmmm... Moist."

Marybelle, intrigued, asked, "How exotic. Is that papaya?"

Sugar, noticing Max had a crumb on his chin, reached over and gently brushed it off, popping it into her mouth. Conrad, in the background, noticed and shifted uncomfortably.

Kitty, curious, asked Florene, "Tell me, did you get this recipe off the side of the Eagle Brand Sweetened Condensed Milk can?"

Florene leaned in, whispering confidentially, "Yes, but I threw in a few personal touches."

"Sure, sure. Who doesn't doctor a recipe?" Kitty agreed, taking another bite. "Gotta make it your own."

As they ate, the atmosphere began to shift. The nervousness seemed to dissipate, replaced by a sense of indulgence and enjoyment. The Identity Bars were a hit, eliciting sounds of appreciation and contentment.

Conrad, clearly enjoying the moment, declared, "These bars are so fantastic and actually, I'm going to vote right now. Best dish tonight!!"

Sugar tried to protest, "But... you haven't tried the others!"

"Something tells me none of them will add up," Conrad responded with a confident grin.

Leslie, holding a tequila glass, agreed, "They taste really great with tequila."

"Give me a shot," Sterling said, downing one quickly. "I agree."

Marybelle, looking a bit dazed, asked, "Why do my eyebrows feel like they're flying off my face?"

Florene smirked, "It's a secret."

Burt, unable to contain his amusement, chuckled. Marybelle, now spinning around playfully, exclaimed, "Oh, glory be! I'm a dancing tree!"

The room swirled with laughter and delight as the effects of the Identity Bars took hold, transforming the earlier tension into a shared, blissful experience. The lines between reality and fantasy blurred as the evening descended into a surreal, euphoric haze.

Everyone indulged in their stoned and drunken stupor. Sterling found a giant decorative banana about two feet long. With a mischievous grin, he pulled off his pants and attached the banana to the front of his underwear, making a grand spectacle of himself.

Max, also stripped down to his underpants and brandishing a giant loaf of bread, couldn't help but play along. "Oh, Sterling, such a big, uh, thingie you have..." Max teased, his eyes glinting with playful mischief.

Sterling, thoroughly enjoying the absurdity of the situation, responded with a hearty laugh, "All the better to split your ass with, my dear..." He swung the banana toward Max, initiating a ridiculous sword fight with their respective props.

"Take that!" Sterling shouted, lunging forward with the banana.

Max parried with the loaf of bread, both men laughing hysterically. Jerome, Sugar, and Burt watched from the sidelines, their own laughter mingling with the chaotic scene. Marybelle, still unsteady from the effects of the night, stumbled over and nearly fell, but Burt was quick to catch her.

"Marybelle, your husband is winning," Sugar called out, her voice laced with amusement.

Marybelle, her senses dulled but her wit still sharp, retorted, "Not with me, he's not."

Sterling, determined to outdo Max, lunged again, this time breaking the loaf of bread in half with his banana. Max looked at the broken loaf in mock despair.

"Shit, what am I gonna do with half a loaf?" he lamented, though his grin betrayed the seriousness of his words.

Marybelle, dropping to her knees, responded with a gleeful shout, "Eat it!" She took a big bite out of the bread, much to the delight of everyone present. The room echoed with laughter, the absurdity of the situation blending with the delirium of their intoxicated state.

As the laughter subsided, the reality of their actions seemed to hang in the air, yet for now, it was drowned out by the roaring merriment. The night had become a whirlwind of ridiculous antics, a surreal blur of laughter, food, and the bizarre, all under the influence of their indulgences.

Conrad was chasing Kitty around the pool, both of them laughing and enjoying the spontaneous fun. As they stopped, Florene emerged from the bushes, topless and holding a fake pistol, adding to the absurdity of the night.

"Freeze!" Florene commanded, affecting a mock serious tone. Conrad and Kitty, caught off guard, stood still. Florene, enjoying the role-play, addressed an imaginary authority figure, "Looks like we got ourselves some no-good hooligans here. Sheriff?"

Leslie, stepping out from behind the bushes in his underwear, played along, "Yes ma'am. Looks like we ought to frisk 'em."

Florene, with exaggerated movements, frisked Conrad, while Leslie approached Kitty with a playful grin. "Ma'am, can you turn down your headlights?" he quipped, nodding to her breasts.

Kitty giggled as Leslie continued the act, "I need to check under the hood," he added, before burying his face in her breasts, much to Kitty's amusement. The group laughed, the earlier tension forgotten in the light-hearted, risqué play.

In the dimly lit bathroom, there was a knock on the door. Sugar, feeling the effects of the night's indulgences, responded, "Just a second." She flushed the toilet and pulled up her panties. Opening the door, she revealed Max standing there in his underwear. He quickly slipped inside and shut the door behind him, creating a small sanctuary from the chaos outside.

Jerome, noticing the secretive movement, stumbled towards the door and pressed her ear against it. She knocked, her voice filled with playful curiosity, "Hey now. Let me come and play too."

Inside the bathroom, Sugar's mouth was inches away from his ears.

Max was thrusting himself into her as she sat on the bathroom sink. Sugar's voice was barely a whisper. "Can you meet me tomorrow?" she asked, her words laced with desperation and hope.

Max, was slightly bewildered and replied, "Yeah, what?"

Jerome's voice persisted from the other side, "Lemme come in and play."

Sugar, ignoring Jerome, leaned in closer to Max, her voice urgent and yearning. "Oh, I can't wait to get you alone. I thought about you all day."

Max was just screwing, not really sure who he was talking to. He responded with, "That's right, baby."

Sugar, filled with emotion, murmured, "Oh, daddy. Take me away from here."

Jerome knocked persistently, her voice muffled but insistent from outside the bathroom door. "Hey you two, stop being so selfish," she called out, her tone a mix of impatience and curiosity.

Inside, Max reached orgasm and his body shook. He

climbed off Sugar as she kissed him passionately.

He grabbed a towel to wipe up the last of the semen dripping from his dick.

Sugar, lost in the moment, looked into Max's eyes, her emotions spilling over. "Oh, I just love you, Max. I love you," she confessed, her voice thick.

Max, a bit unsteady and still processing everything, opened the bathroom door. As he stepped out, he had to maneuver around Jerome, who had now slumped to the floor, unconscious from the night's excesses. The hallway was quiet, save for the soft sounds of music and chatter from the party continuing in the background, as Max stumbled away, leaving Sugar and Jerome behind in their own separate worlds of intoxicated haze.

Kitty, Leslie, and Marybelle were all passed out, sprawled across various pieces of furniture and the floor, remnants of the night's indulgence surrounding them. The room was dimly lit, with only the occasional flicker of a dying candle casting shadows across their faces. Outside, the night air was filled with a strange, almost surreal calmness.

Conrad is engaged with Florene on a lounge chair, taking her from behind, stark and raw. Max stumbled out of the house, his steps uneven, as he approached Florene, positioning himself so she can simultaneously give him a blowjob.

The moment was a frenzy of desperate desires. Burt, standing nearby, watched them with a fond fascination, his hand moving steadily as he masturbated to the threesome unfolding before him.

Inside the house, Conrad walked by Jerome, who lay passed out on the floor, her body limp and unresponsive.

He headed towards the stairs, intending to go to bed, but stopped in his tracks as he saw Sterling on the front lawn, hunched over and vomiting, the sound of retching breaking the night's silence.

Conrad finally reached the bedroom. The room was quiet, almost too quiet. He moved towards the bed, his nude backside briefly illuminated by the hallway light. Without a word, he collapsed onto the empty bed, his body sinking into the mattress. The room remained still as he quickly succumbed to sleep. The house settled into an uneasy quiet.

Chapter 12

The morning air was fresh and vibrant. Birds chirped cheerfully outside the window, their melodies piercing the otherwise silent room. Jerome sat on the edge of the bed, her back rigid, facing the wall. Her posture was tense, her hands clasped tightly together as if holding onto something fragile and intangible.

Leslie sat on the other side, his shoulders slumped, facing away from her. The weight hung heavily between them, an invisible barrier that neither knew how to breach. The room was dense with unspoken words and emotions, the kind that suffocates and lingers long after the silence sets in.

After what felt like an eternity, Leslie's voice broke the stillness. It was soft, hesitant, barely more than a whisper.

"Do you still like me?" he asked, his words hanging in the air like a question meant for someone else.

Jerome didn't respond immediately. Her silence was filled with a myriad of emotions—regret, confusion, anger, and something else she couldn't quite name. She finally stood, the motion slow and deliberate, and walked to the bathroom without a word, leaving Leslie alone in the bedroom's suffocating quiet.

Leslie watched her go, feeling a pang of something deep and aching in his chest. He got up, each step heavy with the burden of his thoughts, and approached the bathroom door. He leaned his forehead against the cool wood, his voice soft and vulnerable.

"I still like you," he said, his voice cracking slightly. "I love you."

He waited, his heart pounding in his chest, but the only response was the sound of the shower turning on. The rush of water was a cold, impersonal answer, one that sent a chill through him. He stood there for a moment longer, listening to the water hit the tiles, before turning and walking away, each step confirming the emptiness that now filled the room.

Leslie left the room, the door closing behind him with a soft click, a sound that felt final and irrevocable. The morning sun streamed through the window, casting a harsh light on the room, revealing the bleak truth of their situation. The birds continued to chirp, their songs incongruent with the heavy silence that now settled over the house, a silence that spoke of things broken and unsaid.

Across the street, Marybelle stood before her mirror, struggling with her hair. No matter how she adjusted it, a stubborn piece kept flipping in the wrong direction, defying her every effort to tame it. Frustration etched across her face, she finally gave up, stomping back into her bedroom with a huff.

Inside, Marybelle sat down at her vanity, staring at her reflection. She pulled her hair back into a ponytail, her movements quick and precise. Then, with a deep sigh, she began the meticulous process of removing her makeup. The foundation, the eyeliner, the carefully drawn eyebrows, and the perfectly painted lips—all wiped away in a single, determined gesture. Her face was bare, raw, and vulnerable, reflecting the deep instability she was trying so hard to suppress.

She started over, applying a fresh layer of foundation, carefully blending it into her skin. She worked on her eyes, adding shadow, liner, and mascara, then moved to her brows, shaping them meticulously. Finally, she applied her lipstick, the color bold and striking against her pale complexion. But as she leaned closer to the mirror, inspecting her work, a wave of dissatisfaction washed over her. Something was off, something she couldn't quite place, but it gnawed at her relentlessly.

With a sharp intake of breath, she grabbed the cloth again, wiping off all the makeup she'd just applied. Tears welled up in her eyes, but she swallowed them down, refusing to let them fall. She forced a smile at her reflection, a brittle, fragile thing that cracked at the edges. It wasn't right. It wasn't perfect. Nothing was.

Marybelle took another deep breath, steadied her hands, and began the ritual once more. Foundation, eyes, brows, lips. Each stroke of the brush was an act of desperation, a frantic attempt to cover the cracks in her facade, to maintain the illusion of control. But the more she tried, the more elusive that perfection became, slipping through her fingers like rainwater.

As she wiped her face clean again, her hands trembled, and she closed her eyes, fighting the rising tide of emotions. The room felt too small, the walls pressing in, and her reflection was a stranger's face. The frustration, the sadness, the overwhelming sense of inadequacy—it all threatened to consume her. But she pushed it down, forced it deep inside, and started over yet again, chasing a perfection she feared she'd never truly find.

In a secluded spot bathed in golden sunlight, Sugar sat on a gingham blanket with a picnic basket. The scene was serene and private, a perfect getaway from the world. The tranquility was interrupted by the sound of a car pulling up behind her. Max stepped out, and they shared a clumsy embrace, a mix of anticipation and uncertainty.

"Pretty isolated out here. Good job," Max remarked, looking around at the solitude. Sugar, eager to please, smiled warmly, explaining, "It's my private spot. I come out here a lot to think. I made us a nice picnic lunch. There's a shooter sandwich and a bottle of Chateau Margaux. Thought it'd be nice to spread out on the ground..."

Max sat down on the blanket, but his demeanor was hurried. "Don't really have the time to eat," he said, his eyes darting around as if searching for something. Sugar, undeterred, continued to pour him a glass of wine, trying to create a moment of connection. "Well, I just thought. I wanted everything to be nice for you. Give you some fuel to fire your ignition."

She poured him a glass, her voice carrying a mix of hope and vulnerability. "When we fooled around, I felt, oh god, I'm going to sound like a teenager, but there was such a bond between us. Like magnetic, right?" Her words hung in the air, seeking affirmation.

Max chuckled softly, pulling her closer, but his actions seemed more driven by the moment than any deep connection. In one fluid movement, he unbuckled his belt, unzipped his fly, unbuttoned her blouse, and lifted her skirt.

"It's like I fell into a trance or something," Sugar continued, her voice softening. "Seriously, I think we fell into another dimension and now we are the only two people in this world. Sugar and Max. If I was still in school I'd write all over my notebooks 'Sugar plus Max'." Her words were cut off as Max started humping her wildly, interrupting her attempts at conversation.

As his thrusts deepened, Sugar's efforts to continue talking were futile. He kissed her, fondling her tits. "The moment you—" she started, but Max was getting more turned on and his kisses prevented her from finishing. "—came to the—" she tried again but gave up as the intensity of the moment took over and they just went at it like animals. The basket of food was forgotten, a wine glass tipped over, spilling onto the blanket. Max repeatedly slid his thick, rock-hard manhood in and out of her welcoming wetness. They were both still half dressed.

After he shot his seed deep inside her, Max immediately stood and began to put his clothes back on. Sugar lay back on the blanket, her skin bathed in the golden sunlight. She mused aloud, "Beedum. Sugar and Max Beedum. Hmmm. Maybe we should go away to Vegas for a few days. What do you think?"

Max, still gathering his thoughts and adjusting his clothes, responded with a hint of hesitation, "Vegas?"

Sugar, with a dreamy tone, suggested, "Why not? It's close enough but far enough so that, you know... a romantic interlude. I read that in a book once. You know, we can eat a nice dinner in a nice restaurant. We could go dancing. I love dancing. I haven't been dancing in...

not since Conny and I first..." She trailed off, reminiscing about a different time.

Max, uncomfortable, said, "I'm no good at it." Sugar, trying to coax him into the idea, reached out, "I don't believe that. Come here." She pulled him close, showing him how to dance, guiding his hands to hold her. "Mmmm. See? You just need to loosen your hips. Relax and enjoy it," she encouraged.

But Max stiffened, his discomfort palpable. "Doesn't feel right," he admitted.

"What do you mean?" Sugar asked, her voice tinged with confusion and a bit of hurt.

Max, pulling away and hastily putting on his shirt, confessed, "I've never danced with anyone but my wife before." The weight of his words hung in the air, a reminder of the complications and boundaries they were both crossing.

Sugar, attempting to shift the mood, mentioned, "You know this wine is very expensive. It's one of the best Bordeauxs you can buy." But Max was already preparing to leave. "I have to get back to the office," he said, kissing her forehead. "Thanks, Sugar."

As he headed toward his car, Sugar called after him, her voice hopeful, "Let's do Vegas. A whole weekend just for us. Think about it." Max gave a noncommittal smile, adjusted his clothes, and left.

Watching him drive off, Sugar turned back to the picnic setup, her emotions a mix of hope and uncertainty. She picked up her wine glass and, with a whimsical air, began to dance around, singing Max's name. "Beedum. Beedum. Beedum," she repeated, twirling and feeling the warmth of the sand beneath her toes, lost in a fleeting moment of fantasy.

Chapter 13

The sun beamed down onto the green as Conrad, Sterling, Leslie, and Burt gathered for their weekly round of golf. They were joined by two new friends, Ned Lavon, a hunky blond athlete, and Gayle Parker, who had bright welcoming eyes. Conrad was at the tee, preparing to swing. The others, dressed in their usual funny golf attire, stood behind him, sipping drinks and chatting.

Sterling leaned in. "Honestly, my favorite thing is when Kitty rubs my monster while I watch *The Carol Burnett Show*," he confessed, grinning mischievously.

Burt chuckled, joining in the banter. "For me, it's *Bewitched*. Can you imagine the kind of orgasm a witch like Samantha could give a man? Mmm, boggles the mind."

Leslie, slightly more reserved, raised an eyebrow. "How is it that our conversations always turn to the subject of sex?" he asked, half-joking.

Ned shrugged, taking a sip of his drink. "People like to talk about the things they want but never get," he said, with a knowing smile.

"Like romance?" Leslie queried, trying to steer the conversation.

"Like blow jobs," Ned corrected, causing a ripple of

laughter among the group.

Sterling nodded in agreement. "Ned, buddy, I'm with you all the way."

Gayle chimed in. "My wife's vagina looks like a parenthesis with an afro," he said, causing a roar of laughter.

Ned shook his head, still chuckling. "I'm not sure I understand vaginas, but I guess we're stuck with them."

Conrad finally took his swing, hitting the ball with a perfect form. He spoke as he watched the ball sail through the air, "What's to understand? A pussy is a doorway. You go in and then you come out. Leslie, you're up, buddy."

Leslie moved to the tee, clearly distracted by the conversation. Ned continued, "Course my wife won't give me a blow job. She won't even consider it. I mean, I go down on her and she's fine with that but when it comes to returning the favor, she's like 'no, no, it's not ladylike.'"

Sterling, licking his lips, remarked sympathetically, "Poor bastard."

Burt added, "You ought to try my wife. She gives the best blow jobs."

The group fell silent for a moment, their eyes shifting between Burt and Conrad. Burt broke the silence, "Just facts. Flo knows what a man needs. Ask Conrad, he's been on the receiving end."

The atmosphere grew tense as all eyes turned to Conrad, who nodded in acknowledgment. "He's right. Flo knows," he confirmed.

Burt continued, explaining their unconventional views. "See, fellas... It's all about symbiosis. The women bring the main course and we provide the dessert. That little Casserole thing they've got going on is a gift just waiting under the tree for us to open."

Gayle, intrigued, asked, "You're talking food and sex? At the same time?"

Leslie, catching on, added, "Chicken a la King... And a pearl necklace."

The men paused, each savoring the thought. Conrad, always the instigator, proposed, "Say, you guys should come over to the house this Friday night. Bring your wives. Will be a lot of fun."

"Really?" Gayle asked, a bit surprised.

Conrad nodded, "Sure, we have to mix around and intermingle if we are going to survive."

Gayle looked puzzled. "Say again?"

Conrad declared, "We have to populate. Populate!"

Just then, Gayle ducked as a golf ball flew past his head, narrowly missing him.

"Oh," Gayle muttered, as the others chuckled.

Sterling, grinning, turned to Ned and said, "It's time to act like ancient Romans."

Burt added, with a sly smile, "Well, something like that."

Ned, catching the spirit, exclaimed, "Magic!"

Conrad raised his flask in the air. The men, raising their drinks, toasted to their unconventional philosophy.

"Grab your clubs, men. It's time to throw our balls around," Conrad declared with a grin.

Leslie mumbled to himself, "I'm uncomfortable with stereotypes."

But the group was already moving on, drinks in hand, their golf clubs rising like scepters from their crotches as they marched down the green, ready for whatever the day—and night—might bring.

Chapter 14

Marybelle stood in front of the mirror, scrutinizing her reflection with a critical eye. Her fingers traced the contours of the dress, a deep shade of blue that contrasted with her pale skin. The fabric hugged her body in all the right places, but there was something that made her uneasy. It was the belt, she decided. The belt hit too high, cutting her silhouette in a way that made her feel... off.

Max emerged from the bathroom, still slightly damp from the shower. He barely glanced at her as he walked by.

"Do you like the way I look in this?" Marybelle asked, her voice tinged with a hint of desperation she tried to mask.

Max paused, not meeting her eyes. "Sure," he replied, his tone nonchalant.

Marybelle's brow furrowed. "What do you mean? Do I look pretty in this dress?"

Max sighed, a familiar frustration bubbling up. "Belle, I've lived with you for twelve years. And I will not fall into your circle conversation."

A flicker of hurt crossed Marybelle's face, quickly replaced by determination. "What are you talking about?

This isn't a circle. This is communication. A simple answer is required, that's all. Just look at me, your wife, and tell me if you like the way I look. This conversation could be over already. Just say yes or no. Please."

Max looked at her then, really looked at her, and felt the weight of her need. "You look delicious. If you were cake, I'd eat you up," he said, forcing a smile.

Marybelle's lips curved into a small, satisfied smile. "There. Now that wasn't so hard, was it?"

She turned back to the mirror, still not entirely convinced. "I don't know though. I think the belt hits me a bit too high. It's like I don't have a waist."

Max, already feeling drained from the exchange, began to leave the room. "Where are you going?" Marybelle called after him, a note of panic creeping into her voice.

"Downstairs where there are no belts," he muttered, rubbing his temples.

Marybelle's eyes filled with tears she refused to let fall. "Lord, you just don't care at all about me, do you? You want your wife to walk around in front of our friends without a waist?"

Max turned, exasperated. "Why not just take the belt off?"

Marybelle stared at him, aghast. "What? And look like a shapeless sack? You are absolutely clueless about fashion."

Max approached her, trying to bridge the growing chasm between them with a kiss, but she pushed him away gently. "Really, Max. I finally got my makeup just right."

As she left the room, her steps quick and decisive, Max stood there, feeling the weight of her words and the chasm widening between them. He felt a deep exhaustion settle over him, not just physical but emotional. It was the kind of tired that sleep couldn't fix, a weariness that came from years of misunderstandings and unmet expectations. As he made his way downstairs, Max couldn't shake the feeling that they were drifting further apart, lost in their separate worlds of unspoken needs and unfulfilled desires.

Chapter 15

That evening, the air buzzed with anticipation as Conrad casually puffed on a cigar, exhaling clouds of rich smoke that hung in the room. Leslie moved with practiced ease, expertly mixing martinis at the bar. The tinkling sound of ice against glass was a familiar and soothing accompaniment to the low hum of conversation.

Sterling stood with an air of pride, introducing his new acquaintances with a flourish. "Kit, I'd like you to meet Ned and Marjorie Lavon. Ned, Marjorie, this is my wife, Kitty."

Kitty smiled warmly, extending her hand. "Nice to meet you," she said, her eyes sparkling with curiosity and friendliness.

Marjorie, a woman of refined elegance, returned the smile. "Likewise," she responded, her voice cultured and soft, as if she'd stepped out of a bygone era.

Conrad, leaning back in his chair with an air of casual authority, greeted the newcomers with a nod, while Leslie handed out the freshly poured martinis, ensuring everyone had a drink in hand. The atmosphere was convivial, yet there was an undercurrent of something more—a subtle tension that only added to the evening's intrigue.

Sterling continued, "And this is Gayle and Patti Parker."

Gayle, a man with an easygoing charm, stepped forward, shaking hands with each of them. "Hi... Hi..." he greeted, his voice enthusiastic yet composed.

Patti, trailing behind him, exuded a quiet grace. She shook hands with Conrad, her eyes taking in the room's decor. "A pleasure. Pleasure," she repeated, her gaze settling on a vase of vibrant hydrangeas that stood proudly on a side table. "Oh, what a lovely home," she remarked, her voice tinged with genuine admiration. She reached out, lightly touching a bloom, her fingers gentle against the delicate petals. "Oh, look at your haciendas, they're so beautiful."

Conrad chuckled softly, pleased by the compliment. "Hydrangeas," he corrected gently, his tone indulgent. "They're one of Sugar's favorites."

The conversation flowed smoothly, each guest slipping into the rhythm of the evening. The night was young, and as the drinks flowed.

Sugar, Florene, and Jerome hovered around a casserole dish.

Sugar was visibly agitated. "I don't know what Conrad has been telling you, but I am fine," she began, her voice edged with frustration. "No, not fine. What does 'fine' even mean? Fine is such a nothing word. I mean, I'm okay. I'm sound. I'm with it. Groovy. Oh God," she sighed, her voice cracking slightly. "See, I tried to be relevant. I just can't sell that, can I? Groovy man. Doesn't feel right coming out of my mouth. What is 'groovy' anyway? I know it's supposed to mean 'good' or even 'fantastic,' but 'I'm groovy' sounds like something a record would say. I mean, if you were to anthropomorphize an album, it would absolutely be right in saying 'I'm groovy.'"

Jerome tried to steer Sugar back to reality. "Sugar, what in the hell are you rambling on about? Here, sit down and take a swig." She handed Sugar a drink, hoping it would calm her nerves.

Taking a sip, Sugar made a face. "Good Lord, Jerome, what is that? Turpentine?"

"Just about. Leslie makes it in the basement," Jerome replied with a smirk, a small hint of pride in her voice.

Florene, intrigued, leaned in. "Leslie has a still?"

"Yes ma'am," Jerome confirmed, her tone nonchalant.

Sugar, still visibly distressed, took another gulp. "Good Lord, Jerome. This isn't the hills of Tennessee. This is a respectable community."

Florene scoffed, "Respectable my ass."

Ignoring the remark, Sugar took another drink, as if trying to drown her confusion and frustration. "Oh screw it. I want to be drunk."

Jerome saw her friend's turmoil and tried to offer some solace. "That's it, Sugar. Just let it all go."

But Sugar was too wrapped up in her thoughts to be soothed. "I mean, who are these people? This was supposed to be just about us. But what are they doing here? They live on the North Side. I don't want to share."

Jerome, always one for mischief, suggested, "Maybe we should sneak off to my house and let them have their own party."

Sugar's eyes flashed with a mixture of defiance and resignation. "That might happen yet."

Florene, eyeing the newcomers, added with a smirk,

"I wouldn't mind trying out either one of them." The comment was met with knowing looks; the boundaries of their relationships had always been fluid, but tonight felt different—more charged, more dangerous.

Jerome, however, remained indifferent. "Not exactly my type."

The tension in the room was interrupted by the arrival of Marybelle and Max. Marybelle set her casserole on the counter, breaking the awkward silence with an overly cheerful, "I made Shepherd's Pie with ground Spam."

Sugar turned to Max, her voice dripping with a mixture of sarcasm and hidden longing. "Hello, Max."

The air in the kitchen thickened, a silence that was filled with all the things they weren't saying. The arrival of Marybelle and Max only underscored the fragility of the evening's facade, each person hiding behind polite smiles and strained laughter, masking the undercurrents of desire, resentment, and unspoken truths that swirled among them.

The mood in the room shifted dramatically as the men gathered around the table. Marjorie Lavon, the only woman present, sat next to her husband Ned, opposite Gayle Parker.

Gayle's voice cut through the room, filled with a bitterness that echoed his discontent. "Damn arthritis. I hate our bodies. Design flaw! That we start failing and die. Who thought that up?" His frustration seemed to reverberate in the stillness of the room.

Marjorie, maintaining her composure, responded with a calm, measured tone. "Well, the Lord God in heaven. He created us."

But Gayle was not to be soothed. "He should have his

license revoked. Giving an expiration date to a consciousness. How cruel. How fucking cruel."

Marjorie, feeling the weight of her beliefs, retorted, "He gave you life too. You can't forget that."

Gayle's anger deepened, his voice growing more intense. "What he gave us is the ability to understand that we are going to die. That is excruciating. My body hurts and it will keep hurting until I stop functioning. Believe in god if it makes you feel better. But if you believe that there is a creator then you have to believe he is the most psychopathic serial killer in all of history. He is the original evil scientist."

The tension in the room was palpable, the men's silence a stark contrast to the intensity of the conversation. Marjorie, unable to continue, excused herself from the table, her departure leaving a void that seemed to amplify Gayle's disturbing words.

Gayle, turning to the men, continued his rant, a dark, almost threatening edge to his voice. "If I killed you right now it wouldn't make any difference would it? Your Father up there, he kills. Must be okay for me to do it too, don't you think?"

Meanwhile, in the kitchen, the mood was similarly strained. Sugar, Kitty, and Marybelle were busy with the casseroles. Florene, sensing something was off, hesitated as Patti approached her.

Patti, with a casual curiosity, asked, "So forgive me for not knowing, but do we take off our clothes now or later?"

Florene, caught off guard but amused, responded, "Whenever you feel like it, hon."

Marjorie, having overheard the exchange, was

horrified. "What in the Good Lord's name are you talking about, Patti?"

Patti, with an innocent expression, clarified, "Well, Gayle didn't tell me if we'd be screwing each other before dinner or after dinner."

Marjorie, her face flushed with embarrassment and anger, stormed out of the kitchen, determined to leave the gathering. Outside by the pool, she confronted Ned, her voice barely restrained. "We are going, Ned. RIGHT NOW."

Ned, taken aback but resolute, refused. "We're not leaving."

Marjorie, desperate to maintain her dignity, pleaded, "NED. Don't do this to me. Not in front of these atheists."

Ned, his voice cold and final, dismissed her. "Go home, Marjorie. Take the car."

Sterling added with a smirk, "We'll give him a ride home."

Marjorie, feeling utterly defeated, turned and walked away, her departure punctuated by Sterling's mocking gesture. As the door closed behind her, the men erupted into laughter.

Conrad, pouring another drink, tried to lighten the mood. "Man, have another drink."

The atmosphere around the table was tense, each guest focused on their meal, avoiding eye contact. The silence was heavy, only broken by the soft clinking of cutlery on porcelain. Ned, left alone by Marjorie, sat stiffly, trying to blend into the background. His eyes flickered nervously between the others, a forced smile plastered on his face as he picked at his food.

Patti, however, was far from uncomfortable. Her eyes

danced with mischief, a sly smile playing on her lips as she scanned the table. Underneath, she discreetly slipped off her shoe and slowly slid her foot up to Leslie's crotch. The unexpected touch made Leslie jerk in surprise, his eyes widening as he struggled to maintain his composure. He nearly choked on his food, coughing awkwardly into his napkin.

Across the table, Patti caught Leslie's eye, a playful, almost daring glint in her gaze. She winked, her foot still gently tracing the pattern of his thickening groin. Leslie's face flushed crimson, a mixture of embarrassment and unexpected excitement washing over him. He glanced around, hoping no one noticed.

The others continued to eat, seemingly oblivious, but the air was charged with an undercurrent of something unspoken, a shared secret lingering just beneath the surface. Ned, feeling out of place, tried to engage in small talk, his voice breaking the uneasy quiet. Yet, the true conversation was happening in the stolen glances, the subtle touches, and the silent, electrifying exchanges that filled the room.

The room felt like a pressure cooker, waiting for a moment to boil over. As the meal continued, each guest was caught in their own thoughts, aware that the evening was far from over and that the real excitement was just beginning.

The group was gathered around the pool, the cool night air mingling with the lingering warmth of the concrete. The water's surface shimmered under the soft glow of the moon, casting a silvery hue over the surface. Everyone was indulging in primal instincts with anyone who walked by. Bodies and flesh entangled, each performing their secret desires.

Sugar stood naked near the edge of the pool, feeling a mix of excitement and unease as Gayle approached her. His eyes were intense, searching hers with an intensity that made her heart race. Gayle reached out, his fingers lightly brushed up her inner thigh and slowly entered her moistness, sending a shiver down her spine. He leaned in, his breath warm against her cheek, and for a moment, Sugar felt herself drawn into his gaze, tempted by the allure of something forbidden. Gayle spread her legs and thrust himself into her like a lion. A rapid set of thrusts is all it took before he was moaning with orgasm and grunting like a wild dog.

Gayle slid himself out of her and stepped back, giving Sugar a chance to breathe. At that moment, Jerome appeared, her eyes soft and understanding. She moved towards Sugar with a grace that felt almost otherworldly, her presence a comforting balm to Sugar's frayed nerves. Without a word, Jerome bent down and kissed Sugar, a gesture filled with tenderness and sincerity.

The kiss deepened, becoming a shared experience of vulnerability and connection. For Jerome, it was a moment of liberation, a chance to be her true self without fear or judgment. The kiss was soft but insistent, and through it, Jerome felt a flood of emotions she had long kept hidden. It was as if, for the first time, she was stepping into the light, shedding the layers of pretense that had kept her bound.

Leslie, who had been caught up in his own world, suddenly looked up. He was wearing a mask to hide his true desires. As he removed the mask, he caught sight of Jerome and Sugar's kiss. The sight struck him like a blow, the authenticity of their connection shining through the haze of superficiality that had clouded the night.

He watched them, a growing sense of anguish filling his heart. The kiss was not just an act of passion; it was a revelation. Leslie saw the raw honesty in their embrace, a stark contrast to the charades they had all been playing. It was a moment of clarity, the truth cutting through the veneer of their carefully constructed lives. Leslie felt exposed, his own insecurities and pretenses laid bare.

As the kiss ended, Jerome and Sugar pulled back, their eyes locked in a silent understanding. Leslie stood frozen, grappling with the realization that he had been living a lie, hiding behind masks and roles. The truth was painful, a sting that left him feeling vulnerable and uncertain.

The group around the pool remained oblivious, caught up in their own spectacles, but for Leslie, the night had taken on a new, sobering significance. The kiss had broken something open, a crack in the facade that would not easily be repaired.

The atmosphere inside the house was charged with a peculiar blend of electricity and heat. The television's flickering light bathed the room in an stimulating glow. Ned, feeling the effects of the booze, stumbled toward the bar, his boxer shorts the only remnant of his earlier attire. He poured himself another drink, the liquid sloshing slightly as his unsteady hands grasped the bottle.

Sterling, equally drunk, approached Ned with a half-lidded gaze, a mischievous grin playing on his lips. "Pour me one too," he murmured, sidling up to Ned and throwing an arm around his shoulders. The two men stood close, the intimacy of their proximity heightened by the low light and the distant murmur of the television.

Ned laughed, a nervous chuckle that seemed to echo in the quiet room. "This is fun, man," he said, though his voice carried an edge of uncertainty. He tipped the bottle, and they watched as the last drops of liquor drained into the glass. "Damn," Ned muttered, frowning at the empty bottle.

Sterling's smile widened. "That's cool. We can share." He took a sip from the glass, then held it up to Ned's lips. Ned hesitated, the drink sloshing slightly, spilling onto his chin and chest. Without missing a beat, Sterling leaned in, his tongue flicking out to lick up the spilled liquid, past Ned's erect nipple to his chin and then lips.

The sensation sent a shiver through Ned, and he turned away, the weight of the moment pressing down on him.

"I don't think I can kiss a man," Ned confessed, his voice barely above a whisper. "I'm a Christian."

Sterling's eyes sparkled with a blend of amusement and challenge. "Me too, man. Christians make the best lovers." He leaned in, capturing Ned's lips in a deep, lingering kiss. There was an intensity to the kiss, a desperation that spoke of long-repressed desires and newfound freedom. Sterling pulled back slightly, their foreheads touching. "Exactly. Remember Judas kissed Christ," he whispered, his breath warm against Ned's skin. "Christ's apostles were all men, for God's sake. What does that tell you?"

Ned's eyes searched Sterling's, looking for reassurance, validation, something to quell the turmoil inside him. "I never thought of it that way," he admitted, the words tumbling out with revelation.

Sterling's smile was soft, encouraging. "Well, start." He closed the distance between them, his lips meeting Ned's in a kiss that was both tender and fierce, a silent promise of acceptance and understanding. As the kiss deepened, Sterling felt Ned's resolve crumble, the barriers he'd erected over a lifetime falling away piece by piece.

In a moment of surrender, Ned kissed him back, hard, with a passion that surprised them both. The room seemed to close in around them, the world outside fading away as they lost themselves in each other. Sterling felt himself being pulled downward, sinking to his knees in front of Ned. He pulled down Ned's shorts and sucked his stiff meaty tool into his eager mouth.

Ned moaned and smiled as Sterling bobbed his head, twisting it back and forth with each downward motion. It didn't take long before Ned was shooting thick ropes of seed into the back of Sterling's throat. Sterling gulped, swallowing every drop. He licked the head clean, and then surprisingly, Ned quickly rolled Sterling backward and bent down to reciprocate.

Sterling's eyes were wide with pleasure. Ned seemed to mimic the same movements, engulfing Sterling's erection with slobbery animalistic hunger. Ned brought his fingers up to play with Sterling's balls as he sucked. Sterling leaned back in pleasure as tears began to form in his eyes. As his cock erupted inside Ned's eager mouth, he closed his eyes and let the tears fall down his cheeks.

In the dimly lit bedroom, Sugar stood before the lamp, her blouse slowly slipping off her shoulders, revealing her bare breasts. The soft glow from the lamp cast her silhouette against the wall, creating a striking and sensual image of her curves. Jerome, with a mix of reverence and desire, adjusted Sugar's position ever so slightly to ensure the shadow was perfect, capturing the essence of her form.

"Yes, right there," Jerome whispered, her voice laced with admiration. She knelt beside the shadow, her eyes fixated on the graceful lines it created. The shadow, larger than life, portrayed a beautiful female form that seemed almost ethereal in the gentle light.

Jerome's hand trembled slightly as she reached out, hesitating for a moment before her fingers made contact with the shadow on the wall. It was a tender touch, as if she feared breaking the spell. "Sugar is sweet and so are you," Jerome murmured, her voice barely more than a breath. Her hand traced the outline of the shadow, a delicate caress that spoke of longing and unspoken emotions.

Outside, Leslie stood by the window, hidden in the darkness. His eyes were fixed on the scene inside, unable to look away. The intimacy of the moment, the quiet reverence with which Jerome touched the shadow, stirred something deep within him. His face was a mask of conflicted emotions—desire, confusion, a profound sadness. As he watched, the reality of his own feelings for Jerome hit him like an asteroid, leaving him breathless and shaken.

Leslie's mouth opened, a silent gasp. The world outside was irrelevant. It was a moment of truth, a revelation.

As he watched Jerome gently caress the outline of Sugar's shadow, the sound of the television in the other room broke through the silence. Leslie turned his head slightly, the words of the news report filtering into his consciousness:

"In a scene described by one investigator as a weird religious homicide - Five persons - including actress Sharon Tate were found dead at the home of Miss Tate and her husband, screen director Roman Polanski..."

The details of the gruesome murders spilled forth, each word like a shard of ice, chilling him to the core. "Miss Tate, who starred in Valley of the Dolls was eight months pregnant and was found in a bikini type nightgown with the rope around her neck, attached to the body of a man. Two bodies inside. Two bodies outside. Among the other victims were Hollywood hairstylist Jay Sebring and coffee heiress Abigail Folger. No one was allowed inside the posh home overlooking Los Angeles. When police arrived, they found the telephone and electricity lines cut."

Leslie was disoriented. It felt as though the world was unraveling, the lines between reality and nightmare blurring until he could no longer tell where one ended and the other began.

His steps were unsteady as he moved through the house. The news report continued:

"The bodies had been dead about twelve hours. They were discovered this morning by a maid who ran screaming to neighbors. One officer summed up the murders when he said, 'In all my years I have never seen anything like this before.'"

Once outside, Leslie crouched down, wrapping his arms around his knees in a fetal position. The sound of the water lapping gently against the sides of the pool.

In the darkness, Leslie reflected on the choices and

circumstances that had led him to this point. "Why did the philosopher drown?" he thought to himself. "Because he jumped in the lake and thought about swimming."

He moved carefully, trying not to disturb the others who were sprawled out around the pool, unconscious or asleep, like marionettes discarded after a frenetic performance.

As Leslie made his way around the pool, he caught a glimpse of his own reflection in the water. For a moment, he was startled—the face staring back at him seemed foreign, detached, as if belonging to someone else. The reflection, bathed in the pale moonlight, appeared to smile, a faint, eerie grin that sent a chill down his spine. Leslie leaned in closer, mesmerized, and noticed something unusual at the bottom of the pool.

A dark shape lay submerged, its outline becoming clearer as Leslie squinted through the water. With a sudden burst of energy, he dove in, the cold water shocking his senses awake. He swam downward, the water pressure building against his ears as the mysterious object came into focus. It was a mask, large and vividly colored, painted in luminous shades that seemed to glow in the dark depths.

Leslie reached out and grasped the mask, feeling its smooth surface under his fingers. As he brought it closer, the design became more apparent—a beautifully crafted fish, its scales detailed and intricate. He marveled at the craftsmanship, the colors almost surreal in their brightness underwater. Impulsively, he slipped the mask over his face.

A strange sense of liberation bathed him. Leslie felt light, free, as if the mask had somehow lifted the weight of his anxieties and doubts. He swam around the pool, moving with an uncharacteristic grace, his legs fluttering and arms cutting through the water with fluid ease. The water felt like silk against his skin, and for the first time in a long while, Leslie felt a genuine sense of joy.

From beneath the water's surface, he looked up at the moon, a glowing orb in the dark sky that danced on the rippling surface above him. Leslie felt at peace, a calm he hadn't known he needed until now. He swam closer to the surface, drawn toward the light, feeling the water embrace him in a cool, soothing cocoon.

As he neared the top, the world seemed to shift. The peaceful scene transformed; the joyful swimming took on a more frantic, desperate energy. His movements slowed, the once silken water now felt heavy and resistant. Leslie's breaths came shorter, his vision blurred by the mask and the water's distortion. He reached out, trying to grasp something, anything, but his hands only met the empty, cold water.

Suddenly, his body went limp, and he floated to the surface. The fish mask remained on his lifeless face. From above, Leslie's body appeared almost serene, face down in the water, the mask obscuring his features. Around him, the scene was eerily calm, the other guests oblivious in their slumber, scattered like fallen leaves.

The water, now still, held him gently, a final embrace in the silent, empty night.

Chapter 16

The morning sun peeked over the horizon. The couples were still scattered around in various stages of undress. Kitty stirred first, her body protesting the movement. Her eyes squinted against the harsh light, and she rubbed her temples, the throbbing headache of a hangover making itself known.

As she slowly became more aware of her surroundings, she noticed her blouse draped over a chair nearby. She reached for it, fumbling slightly, her fingers still clumsy from sleep and too much alcohol. She slipped it on, the fabric cool against her skin, and stood up, only to realize she was still in her panties. Her eyes darted around, a mix of embarrassment and disorientation on her face.

"Jesus. Deja vu," Kitty muttered to herself, the absurdity of the situation not lost on her. She began to walk around, her steps tentative as she tried to piece together the events of the night before. Her surroundings slowly came into sharper focus—the overturned glasses, the scattered clothes, the faint scent of chlorine mingling with stale alcohol.

As she approached the edge of the pool, Kitty stretched, trying to shake off the lingering fog in her head. She glanced down at the water, expecting to see her reflection, but instead, her eyes widened in horror. A blood-curdling scream tore from her throat, piercing like an alarm.

There, just breaking the surface of the water, was Leslie's dead body. His skin had turned a sickly blue, and a thin streak of red streamed from a wound on his head, staining the water around him. The sight was grotesque.

Kitty's scream jolted the others awake, their groggy states quickly replaced by shock and horror. They rushed over to Kitty, their faces pale and eyes wide as they took in the scene before them. Gasps and cries filled the air, the realization of what had happened settling in.

Burt, his voice thick with panic, shouted, "Call an ambulance!" His words hung in the air, an urgent command that none of them followed.

Jerome, moving almost mechanically, stumbled to the edge of the pool. She looked down at Leslie in a complete daze. Slowly, she sank to her knees, her body folding in on itself as if trying to shield her from the experience before her. She reached out, her hand trembling, and took hold of Leslie's cold, limp hand. She laid her head on the pool's edge, her hair splaying out on the tiles, and just held his hand, silent tears streaming down her face.

The others stood around, their sobs and cries mixing with the sounds of the morning. Some clung to each other, seeking comfort, while others stood apart, stunned and silent. The bright, cheerful morning had turned into a scene of mourning and despair.

Jerome remained by the pool, her body shaking with silent sobs. She couldn't bring herself to look away from Leslie's face, his once lively eyes now closed, his mouth slightly open as if caught mid-sentence.

Leslie was gone, and nothing would ever be the same again. The sun climbed higher in the sky, the day growing warmer even as their world grew colder.

Chapter 17

The couples were dressed in black, their faces marked with the solemnity of the occasion. The kitchen counter was laden with casseroles, an almost absurdly large assortment that reflected the community's tradition of comfort food in times of grief.

Sugar, Marybelle, and Kitty were huddled together, assembling yet another casserole, their hands moving mechanically, more out of habit than necessity. The silence among them was punctuated only by the occasional clink of utensils and the quiet, measured sips of bourbon from Jerome, who sat apart from the group. Dressed in a sharp, fitted black Edwardian suit, Jerome was an island of quiet, her eyes fixated on the small television screen before her.

"What's Jerome doing over there?" Sugar asked, her voice barely above a whisper, as if afraid to break the fragile stillness that hung over them.

"She's playing a drinking game," Florene responded, her tone flat. "Anytime someone says 'groovy' on TV, she takes a drink."

"We better watch her close," Sugar muttered, concern creeping into her voice.

Jerome, seated too close to the flickering screen,

watched a sitcom scene unfold—a 60s teenage boy and girl, their dialogue innocuous yet painful in its simplicity.

"You wanna go to the movies with me, Betty?" the boy asked.

"Yeah, Johnny. That would be groovy," the girl responded.

Jerome took a deep swig from the bottle of bourbon, her eyes never leaving the screen.

"Wow, Betty. I mean, groovy," the boy repeated, prompting another gulp from Jerome.

In a corner, Marybelle scrutinized her reflection in a compact mirror, her brow furrowed in worry. "Kitty, does my face look red to you?" she asked, her voice tinged with insecurity.

Kitty, busy stirring a bowl, glanced over briefly. "Oh, Marybelle, you're always so concerned with your face. Why not take a break from that mirror and give me a hand with the casserole?"

Marybelle hesitated, her fingers tracing the rim of the compact. "I must have gotten too much sun when I was reading by the pool yesterday. Funny though, I was wearing a hat."

Kitty reached over and snapped the compact shut with a sigh. "Put down your wand, Sorceress, and open some soup for me."

As Marybelle picked up a can opener, she paused, a curious look crossing her face. "Do you think angels hide in our hair?"

Sugar looked up, puzzled. "Marybelle?"

"Angels," Marybelle repeated, her voice dreamy. "Do you think they hide in our hair? I think angels are real tiny and transparent, and they hide in our hair and sometimes sit and dangle their feet off the top of our ears so that they can give us advice when we're having troubles."

The room fell silent. Marybelle opened a can of cream of mushroom soup, turning it over and pushing the contents onto a plate, the solid gel-like soup wobbling slightly.

Sterling, Max, and Burt entered, their faces a mix of confusion and amusement. "What in the hell is that?" Sterling asked, his voice breaking the spell.

"Jesus. Is that solid soup?" Max added, peering at the plate with a mixture of fascination and disgust.

Marybelle looked at them, her eyes wide. "You know perfectly well what this is. We cook with it all the time."

Burt chuckled, shaking his head. "How do they get the soup to hold its shape like that?"

Kitty, her voice breaking slightly, murmured, "I miss Leslie's voice."

Jerome, seemingly oblivious to the conversation around her, muttered to herself, "I want to be with my husband. I want to have sex with my husband! I can do the headstand, Lessie. Is that what you want? I can do the headstand."

Jerome stumbled towards the wall, grabbing a cushion and tossing it to the floor. "Oh, damn. These pants aren't gonna work. I can't do a headstand in these pants."

Before anyone could stop her, Jerome stripped off her pants, standing naked from the waist down. "Jerome?..." Sugar started, her voice filled with concern.

Jerome waved her hand dismissively, positioning herself against the wall and attempting a headstand. "C'mon, Lessie, raise my consciousness," she muttered, her voice slurred.

Marybelle rushed over, grabbing Jerome's pants from the floor. "Get down, Jerome," she pleaded, trying to pull her friend back to the ground.

With Sugar's help, they managed to get Jerome dressed again. "Stop that," Sugar chided gently, pulling the pant leg on.

Jerome, still in a daze, leaned in towards Sugar. "Hooray, Sugar wants a repeat," she mumbled, leaning in for a kiss. Sugar pushed her away, her face a mix of pity and concern.

Conrad, watching from the doorway, shook his head slowly. "What a mess," he muttered, his voice tinged with disgust.

Chapter 18

After the wake, the atmosphere in the house was suffocating, filled with the weight of death. Sugar stood in the kitchen, methodically cleaning up. The casserole she had prepared—a dish she had hoped would bring some comfort—sat cooling on the stove. She moved with a robotic efficiency, her mind far away from the mundane task at hand.

Conrad entered, the sharp scent of alcohol preceding him. His eyes were glassy, a mix of anger and weariness that had become all too familiar. He was a storm barely contained.

"Sit down, Conny, and I'll get you your dinner. I made your favorite!" Sugar's voice was overly bright, a thin veneer of cheerfulness that barely masked her anxiety. She gestured toward the casserole, hoping to bridge the widening gap between them.

Conrad took a swig from his drink, his expression hardening. "Another bubbling concoction of crap. Why can't we ever have a real meal?" His words were laced with disdain, striking Sugar like physical blows.

Her face fell, the forced smile slipping away. "But this is Turkey Divan Strata. You love this. I made it for you the first night we moved into this house, remember?" Her voice was soft, almost pleading, as she tried to remind him of happier times.

Conrad's eyes narrowed. "Steak would be a good meal," he said, his tone dismissive.

Sugar turned away, her hands trembling as she folded a towel. She took a long drink from her martini, trying to steady herself. "This has turkey in it and spinach—" she began, but Conrad cut her off.

"I'm sick of this bullshit you concoct out of canned crap. You're too lazy to cut up some real vegetables and grill me a piece of meat?" His voice rose, the anger bubbling over. "Sterling says Kitty makes a different meal every night," he continued, his voice dripping with sarcasm.

Sugar flinched, the words cutting deep. "Kitty's not very creative," she retorted weakly, trying to deflect the criticism.

But it was no use; Conrad was relentless. "What about a roast chicken? I would love a roast chicken."

The mention of Kitty hit a nerve. "Kitty is my friend, but she is not roasting chickens. Believe me, she couldn't bake a potato," Sugar snapped, the tension making her defensive.

Conrad sneered. "You don't even try. You do nothing. Hell, even the can opener does the work for you." His words were a brutal assessment, stripping away any pretense of civility.

Sugar's eyes welled with tears. "Today was about Leslie; I didn't have time to truss a bird for you," she said, her voice breaking.

Conrad mimicked her, his tone mocking. "'I didn't have time...' You are a stupid little hole, you know that?" He drained his drink and moved to the liquor cabinet for a refill, his movements jerky and aggressive.

Sugar's composure cracked. "Conny, I saw you. I saw you screwing that bitch. You were enjoying it," she said, her voice trembling with a mix of hurt and anger. "Is it easier with a stranger? Is that what you like?"

Conrad's face darkened. "Do you really want to get into this now?" he asked, his voice low and dangerous.

Sugar nodded, her eyes blazing. "You should have never invited those people here. They had nothing to do with our group."

Conrad laughed bitterly. "You mean they had nothing to do with you and Max Beedum," he shot back, his words laced with accusation.

Sugar recoiled, stunned. "What do you mean?"

"Come on, Sugar. Be honest. You've been wet for Max since they moved across the street. I know how that deceitful mind of yours works. You couldn't wait to get Max inside you. You planned that party and got us all drunk so you would have an excuse to live out your fantasy," Conrad spat, the venom in his voice palpable.

Sugar shook her head, tears streaming down her face. "That isn't true," she whispered, but the conviction in her voice was gone.

"The hell it isn't!" Conrad yelled, his rage boiling over.

"You twist everything around," she said. "There's no way to get through to you."

"Shut your fucking mouth. For chrissakes," he shouted, his face twisted in fury. Conrad stood abruptly, shoving his chair into the table with a loud bang. He poured himself another drink, his hands shaking with anger.

Sugar's tears flowed freely now, her shoulders shaking with silent sobs. She moved to the stove, retrieving a plate from the cabinet. "Would you like one scoop or two?" she asked, her voice hollow.

For a moment, Conrad stared at her, his expression unreadable. Then, with a sudden, violent motion, he shoved the casserole off the stove. The dish shattered on the floor, its contents spilling out in a messy, steaming heap.

"I DON'T WANT YOUR FUCKING CASSEROLE!" Conrad roared, his voice echoing through the kitchen. He took another swig of his drink, the alcohol doing nothing to dull his anger.

Sugar fell to her knees, sobbing openly. She began scooping up the ruined food, placing it back into the shattered casserole dish. Her hands were shaking, her tears mingling with the food.

Conrad stood over her, his face a mask of cold disdain. "I'm sick of it. I'm sick of you. I'm sick of this house. I'm sick of your whiny mouth. I'm sick of your excuses. The Sugar I married is long gone. I feel like I'm married to a corpse," he said, his voice devoid of any warmth.

Sugar looked up at him, her eyes red and swollen. "I made dinner. This was your favorite dinner. It isn't easy to make. I thought you'd like it. I try really hard to make you happy. But you ruin it. You always ruin it. You get drunk and you get mad. And you lock yourself in the bathroom and you do that awful thing you do to yourself. Your legs are like raw hamburger meat. How am I supposed to love that?" she cried, her voice breaking with emotion.

Conrad stared at her, his eyes cold and unfeeling. "You don't know what you're talking about," he muttered, turning away.

Sugar's voice was barely a whisper. "Conny. I'm pregnant."

The words hung in the air, heavy and charged. Conrad turned back to her, his face a mask of shock. For a moment, there was silence, broken only by Sugar's sobs.

Conrad's face twisted into a sneer. "Whore," he said, his voice low and dangerous.

Sugar flinched as if struck. Conrad moved closer, his eyes blazing with anger. "Isn't that an ugly word? Whore. I think it's the hard H sound. Huh. Huh. Followed by that hard R. Rrrr. Whore. Whore. Really ugly, don't you think? You almost have to expectorate to say it. WHORE. That's what makes it such a horrible word. Not just the consonants hitting each other, are you with me? But that it takes some energy to say it. Whore! You really have to push to get it out. Whore. Whore. Whore," he spat, his voice rising with each repetition.

He grabbed Sugar, pulling her into a tight embrace. But there was no love in the gesture, only a desperate, painful need. He squeezed her so tightly that she struggled to breathe, her face a mask of fear and confusion.

Conrad held her for a moment longer, then abruptly let go. He turned and stormed out of the room, slamming the door behind him. Sugar stood there, gasping for breath, her hands still clutching a broken piece of the casserole dish. She stared after him, her mind a whirlwind of emotions—fear, sadness, anger, and an overwhelming sense of despair.

Chapter 19

Jerome woke up, the morning light casting a golden glow through the cacti outside the window. She rolled over, reaching out instinctively, but her hand found only the cold, empty pillow beside her. The sight of the vacant space sent a wrench through her chest, stirring memories that felt as real as if they were happening again.

She remembered Leslie standing in front of their full-length mirror, clad only in his underwear. He was poking and prodding at his body, his face twisted in a mix of self-criticism and resignation. He grabbed at the soft flesh around his stomach and sides, his fingers pressing into the skin as if trying to reshape it.

"I'm a lemon, Jerome. I am a bag of Jello. Look at me, I'm the Yeti," Leslie had said, his voice heavy with disdain. Jerome could still hear the way he chuckled bitterly, masking his discomfort with humor.

She had walked up behind him then, wrapping her arms around his middle, feeling the warmth of his skin against hers. "Oh, shut up. I like you just fine the way you are," she had murmured, pressing a kiss to his shoulder. But Leslie had only shaken his head, his eyes locked on their reflection.

"No one likes a man with ballast," he had muttered, his voice tinged with a sadness that cut through Jerome. She remembered the frustration, the helplessness that had bubbled up inside her. She had loved Leslie so deeply, with a fierce protectiveness, and it pained her to see him so consumed by self-doubt.

In a bid to comfort him, to prove that she understood, she had stripped off her clothes, standing beside him in her underwear. "There. Look at me. I'm not exactly a tasty dish," she had said, her voice firm. She had hoped that by baring herself, by showing him her own insecurities, she could bridge the gap between them.

But Leslie had only turned his gaze from the mirror to her, his eyes softening. "What are you talking about? You are the most beautiful woman I've ever seen," he had said, his tone earnest. Yet, even as he spoke, he continued to critique himself, calling himself a "manatee with male pattern baldness. God, when did this happen? I'm not a man anymore."

"Of course you're a man. You're my man," Jerome had insisted, her voice breaking with emotion. But Leslie had shaken his head, refusing to be consoled. "No, I'm not. I'm a dump truck, a cruise liner. I'm the darn Isthmus of Panama."

"You're perfect to me," she had whispered, the words spilling out with a raw, desperate honesty. She had meant it with every fiber of her being. To her, Leslie was more than his body; he was her partner, her confidant, the love of her life.

Now, back in the present, Jerome clung to that memory, the pain of his absence a physical ache in her chest. She buried her face in Leslie's pillow, inhaling deeply as if trying to capture the last remnants of his scent. Tears welled in her eyes, spilling over and soaking into the fabric. She hugged the pillow tightly, as if it were Leslie himself, as if holding it could somehow bring him back.

"You're perfect to me," she whispered, her voice choked with sobs. The emptiness of the room pressed in around her. The weight of her grief was crushing, a heavy blanket that smothered her, leaving her feeling hollow and lost.

Jerome stayed there for what felt like hours, the tears flowing freely as she let herself feel the full extent of her loss. It was a raw, visceral pain, one that cut deep and left her gasping for breath. She had lost more than just a partner; she had lost a part of herself, a piece of her heart that she knew she could never get back.

Jerome finally forced herself to get up. She wiped her eyes, taking a deep, shuddering breath. The day stretched out before her, a daunting expanse of time that she would have to fill without Leslie by her side. But even in her despair, she knew that she had to keep going, if only to honor the love they had shared.

With trembling hands, Jerome began to gather up Leslie's things, each item a painful reminder of the man she had lost. She folded his clothes, packed away his belongings, and tried to find some semblance of closure. But the pain remained, a dull, throbbing ache that she knew would never fully go away.

"You're perfect to me," she repeated softly. The words echoed in the empty room.

Chapter 20

Kitty stood by the laundry basket, meticulously folding the last pair of socks. The rhythmic task of folding clothes often gave her a sense of calm, a momentary escape from the whirl of daily life. She neatly placed the freshly laundered items into the basket, each piece a small token of domestic normalcy.

As she made her way to the bedroom, the faint glow from Sterling's den caught her eye. It was unusual for the light to be left on, especially since Sterling was meticulous about such things. Kitty set down the basket, her curiosity piqued, and walked into the den to turn off the light.

Her hand hesitated over the switch as something under the desk caught her attention. A gym bag, haphazardly shoved beneath, had a dirty sock peeking out from the top. Kitty frowned, the sight of the sock jarring against the otherwise orderly room. She bent down and pulled the bag out, intending to add the sock to the laundry pile.

As she reached inside to retrieve the sock, her fingers brushed against something unexpected. She froze, her breath catching in her throat as she pulled out a stack of photographs. The glossy prints slipped through her fingers, revealing images of nude men posed in various positions. Some were simply standing, their expressions blank or seductive, but others were more explicit, showing intimate acts between two men.

Kitty's heart raced, a mix of confusion and disbelief clouding her thoughts. She flipped through the photos, each image blurring into the next. The shock of the discovery left her numb, her mind struggling to make sense of what she was seeing. These photos, hidden away in Sterling's den, were a world apart from the life she thought they shared.

Her hands trembled as she placed the photos back into the bag, careful to tuck the dirty socks on top, just as she had found them. Kitty stood up, her gaze lingering on the gym bag for a moment longer, as if trying to imprint the reality of what she had found into her mind.

She turned, leaving the den with the sock in hand, and picked up the laundry basket. The weight of the clothes felt heavier now, a physical burden mirroring the emotional one that settled over her. Kitty continued down the hallway, her steps slow and measured, as she tried to process the revelation.

In the quiet of the house, her thoughts raced. Had she missed something? Were there signs that she had overlooked? The photographs were not just a random discovery; they were a window into a part of Sterling's life that she had never seen, never even suspected. Kitty felt a pang of hurt and betrayal, not just for the hidden secrets, but for the realization that there were parts of Sterling she did not know at all.

As she entered the bedroom and began putting away the laundry, Kitty's movements were mechanical, her mind elsewhere. The basket emptied, but her thoughts remained full of questions. She glanced at herself in the mirror, searching for answers in her own reflection, but finding none.

The day continued on, the house filled with the usual sounds of life, but for Kitty, everything had changed. The discovery in the den was a reminder that even in the most familiar places, secrets could lie hidden. She knew she couldn't ignore what she had found, but she also wasn't sure how to confront it. As she finished the last of the laundry, Kitty resolved to keep the secret for now, unsure of what the future would hold, but certain that things could never be the same again.

Chapter 21

Sugar stood by her kitchen window, her face reflected in the glass like a ghost. She wore a yellow frock with a ruffle around the neck. It was as if she were a flower in bloom, trying to outshine the storm clouds of doubt and fear swirling inside her.

Across the street, she watched Marybelle emerge from her house and get into her car. Sugar's eyes tracked every movement, her heart pounding in her chest. As soon as Marybelle drove off, Sugar's body sprang into action, propelled by a desperate urgency.

Dashing to the door, she left her house, casting cautious glances up and down the street, as if expecting someone to stop her. The world around her felt muted, her focus narrowed to a single point: Max.

Max opened the door, wearing gym clothes, sweat glistening on his brow.

"Hey Sugar, Marybelle just left?" he greeted, a hint of confusion in his voice.

Sugar didn't respond to his question. Instead, she pushed past him into the house, her mind racing. "Oh, Max. I missed you," she said, moving to kiss him, her voice trembling with emotion. The scent of his sweat mingled with her own anxiety, a mix of desire and desperation.

Max kept her at arm's length, his brow furrowed. "Just got back from a run," he explained, as if his words could explain away the emotional intensity radiating from Sugar.

Ignoring his attempt to distance himself, Sugar pressed on, her words tumbling out in a rush. "Max, how long will it take you to pack? We can take my car. I already have my bags in the trunk. If we leave now, we can get to Vegas by nightfall."

Her eyes sparkled with a manic hope, her hands reaching for him as if he were her only lifeline. But Max pulled away, his face a mask of disbelief. "Sugar, what are you talking about?"

"I'm having our baby!" Sugar's voice was high-pitched, teetering on the edge of hysteria. She smiled, expecting joy, excitement, any positive response from Max.

But Max's face fell, shock and confusion warring in his eyes. "How do you know it's mine?" he asked, the words falling like stones between them.

Sugar's smile wavered, but she pressed on, desperate to make him understand. "That day on the picnic blanket. That's when it happened. I knew right away. I felt alive for the first time in years."

Max's eyes darted around, searching for an escape, a way out of this conversation that felt like quicksand. "Sugar, we were just having some fun. We were drunk. You probably forgot and this is someone else's mistake..."

"Mistake?!?" The word cut through Sugar like a knife. Her face paled, the brightness of her dress mocking the despair that settled in her eyes. "Max, I love you... And you love me. You met me in secret. That was different. That was special."

Max looked away, unable to meet her gaze. "I'm sorry. I love Marybelle. She's my wife. And I'm not going to leave her. Not now. Not ever."

The finality in his voice shattered the last of Sugar's hopes. Her hands fell to her sides, the light in her eyes dimming. "But we are a family now. You're going to be a daddy."

Max shook his head, the distance between them growing with each passing second. "You were with the other guys, too. I saw you. Everybody was doing everyone. So that kid could belong to your husband or you know, Burt, Sterling... Maybe it's Leslie's..."

"No, this is our baby. Conny hasn't touched me in eons. And I didn't, the others... You were the only one I let finish... Weren't you...?" Sugar's voice broke, her words unraveling like a frayed thread.

Max's expression hardened, a wall going up between them. "We were just playing."

The air thickened, pressing down on them. Sugar stood there, frozen, unable to process the reality crashing down around her. Max reached out to touch her shoulder, but she recoiled, flicking his hand away as if it burned her.

"It's okay. I'm okay," she muttered, her voice hollow. She turned to leave, but stopped at the door, looking back at Max one last time. "What am I supposed to do, Max? What am I supposed to..."

Max, unable to look her in the eye, simply said, "You'll figure it out, Shug."

As the door closed, Sugar felt a cold emptiness settle over her. Her reflection in the shiny brass door knocker looked faded and wilted, like a flower left too long in the sun. She stood there for a moment, staring at her own distorted image, before turning away and walking back across the street, each step feeling heavier than the last. The world around her distorted, her vision narrowing to a tunnel of despair and confusion.

Sugar's steps faltered as she walked across the driveway, each footfall heavy with the weight of her shattered dreams. Her gaze was distant. As she reached her front door, she paused, her hand hovering over the handle. Her knuckles turned white as she gripped the handle, holding onto it as if it were the only thing keeping her grounded.

She stood there, her heart pounding in her chest, her breath shallow. The seconds stretched into an eternity, and the world seemed to hold its breath with her. The silence was deafening. She felt as though she were standing on the edge of a precipice, teetering on the brink of an abyss she couldn't quite see but could feel in the pit of her stomach.

Finally, with a deep breath, Sugar pushed the door open. The effort seemed monumental. She stepped inside, the bright door closing behind her with a soft click. The sound echoed in the empty house, a final punctuation to the end of her illusions. Sugar stood in the dim light of the hallway, her heart heavy with the realization that everything she had hoped for was slipping through her fingers. The silence inside the house was oppressive, amplifying the loneliness that wrapped around her like a cloak.

A single tear traced down her cheek. She felt hollow, as if the vibrant, hopeful person she had been was now just a ghostly echo in an empty shell.

For a long moment, she stood there, her body still and her mind racing. She felt the crushing weight of her own vulnerability, the realization that she was utterly alone in this moment. Her breath came in ragged gasps, the air around her thick with the taste of despair.

Finally, she pushed herself away from the door, her movements slow and deliberate. The house felt like a prison, its walls closing in around her. She took a step forward, then another, her feet dragging as the weight pulled her down.

As she moved through the house, the silence was broken only by the soft sound of her footsteps. Sugar's shoulders slumped, her head bowed, as she made her way to the living room. She sank into the couch, her body curling into itself to hide from the world.

The tears came then, silently at first, then in great, heaving sobs that shook her entire body. She buried her face in her hands, her fingers tangling in her hair as she cried. The grief was overwhelming, a tidal wave of emotion that crashed over her, leaving her gasping for breath.

Sugar's sobs were the only sound, a raw, visceral expression of pain. She wept for the loss of her dreams, for the love she had never truly had, for the life that had slipped through her fingers.

Chapter 22

Kitty was on her knees on the kitchen counter, methodically cleaning every inch of the cabinets. It wasn't just cleaning; it was an intense, obsessive ritual, as if scrubbing away the grime could somehow bring clarity to her chaotic thoughts. Sterling entered the room, his presence breaking the silence.

"Hey S. How was your day?" Kitty asked, her tone deceptively light.

"Long," Sterling replied, setting down his briefcase. He moved to the bar, his hands already reaching for a drink, seeking comfort in the familiar ritual of pouring whiskey.

Kitty continued, her voice steady, "I did laundry today. Got through two loads before I found the dirty gym clothes in your den." Her words were casual, but there was an undercurrent of something more.

Sterling froze, his back to her, a sudden wave of panic washing over him. His face, unseen by Kitty, was a mask of dread.

"I went ahead and washed them for you, dried them, and I put them back where I found them," she continued, her voice calm but pointed. Kitty dipped her cloth into a tub of bleach water, scrubbing the inside of a cabinet with meticulous care. Her focus was absolute, the scene framed from the inside of the cabinet, highlighting her intensity.

"I'm happy to do your laundry, darling," she added, her voice taking on a sweeter tone. "But I can't clean dirty clothes I don't know about." She jumped off the counter, her movements smooth, and planted a kiss on his cheek, her gesture affectionate yet laden with unspoken accusations.

"Next time try and remember to put them in the dirty clothes basket. Okay?" Her tone was light, almost teasing, but Sterling remained motionless, staring forward, lost in his own turmoil. Kitty walked out of the room, peeling off her rubber gloves, her steps measured and calm.

"I have a couple steaks marinating for dinner. Shall we eat out on the patio? It's going to be a beautiful night. Full moon," she called out, her voice carrying a strange cheerfulness. Through the kitchen doorway, she glanced up at the sky through the bay window.

Sterling stood still and silent in the doorway. "Sure," he finally responded, his voice cracking slightly.

Kitty turned to go upstairs, her steps echoing with a deliberate rhythm. "I'm gonna get changed. Will you run to the liquor store and pick up a bottle of wine?" she asked, her voice disappeared as she climbed the stairs.

Sterling stood frozen, a cold sweat breaking out across his forehead. The room felt suddenly too small. Kitty's footsteps pounded in his ears, each step amplifying the sense of impending doom. He reached for his keys, his hand trembling slightly, as he prepared to escape the suffocating atmosphere of the house, if only for a brief moment. The door clicked shut behind him, leaving the kitchen in a heavy silence, the scent of marinating steaks lingering in the air.

Sterling paid for his wine and headed out of the store, his mind preoccupied. As he exited, he bumped into Ned, accompanied by another man. Sterling greeted him enthusiastically, "Hey, buddy!" However, Ned barely acknowledged him, quickly moving past as if they were strangers. Sterling, taken aback, watched Ned walk away, puzzled by the cold reception.

Sterling stood by his car, waiting, trying to piece together the sudden shift in Ned's demeanor. Moments later, Ned reemerged from the store, and Sterling called out to him again, this time with more urgency, "Hey, Ned, come here a sec."

Ned waved off his companion and approached, his expression tense. "What do you want?" he asked, a defensive edge to his voice.

Sterling, still confused, tried to bridge the gap. "What's going on, Ned?" he asked, seeking clarity.

Ned glanced around nervously, "I'm on my way someplace. I gotta go."

Sterling, sensing something was amiss, leaned in closer, lowering his voice, "I thought maybe you might want to get together sometime."

Ned's reaction was swift and harsh, his voice tight with anger and embarrassment. "Hey man, I'm not that way."

Sterling, feeling both confusion and hurt, pressed on, "For not being 'that way', you give an awesome blow job, buddy."

Ned's face flushed red with a mix of anger and shame. Without warning, he swung his fist, connecting hard with

Sterling's face, sending him sprawling to the ground. "Stay away from me!" Ned spat, his voice shaking with rage.

Sterling, stunned and in pain, slowly pulled himself up, blood dripping from his nose. He leaned against his car, the realization of what just happened sinking in. He watched helplessly as Ned walked away, quickly getting into his car and driving off without a backward glance.

As Sterling struggled to process the encounter, the wine bottle slipped from his hands, shattering on the pavement. Some of the wine spurted, landing on his white pants.

Chapter 23

Jerome sat at the outdoor table, draped in a pink satin tuxedo, a striking sight under the moon's silvery gaze. The table was meticulously set for two, with fine china, polished silverware, and crystal glasses. Opposite her, Leslie's caftan lay spread across the chair, an empty echo of his presence. Jerome raised her glass in a solemn toast to the empty fabric, the full moon's glow casting a soft blue hue over the scene.

The moon hung low and luminous, its cratered face clearly visible in the night sky. Jerome, filled with a mix of sadness and defiance, looked up, addressing the celestial body as if it were a familiar companion.

"Hey moon," she called out, her voice full of longing, "What are you looking at? Hey, hey. I got a limerick for you. Okay, okay. Here goes." She cleared her throat, reciting with a bitter edge, "The man who chose to melt, He felt everything he felt, He stood in his room which was really his tomb, 'cause he chose to drip where He dwelt."

The moonlight seemed to intensify, bathing her in its ethereal glow. Jerome's voice softened, tinged with a desperate yearning, "Isn't that a stinger? I'm a wordsmith. A little cuntie wuntie. You got my Leslie up there with you? He took a powder and fled to your craters, didn't he? Son of a bitch. Chicken shit. Went for a swim and got abducted by the Man in the Moon. You take care of him, Moon Man. He's a good kid."

With a fragile smile, Jerome walked over to the caftan, gently picking it up. She held the soft fabric close, its texture a cold reminder of Leslie's absence. As if driven by some unseen force, she began to dance, twirling under the moon's gaze, the caftan fluttering around her like wings. Her movements were slow, dreamlike, each step a whispered prayer for Leslie's return.

"I'm gonna get you, Leslie. I'm gonna get you," she murmured, her voice growing louder with each repetition. In a sudden burst of energy, she ran to a nearby tree and began to climb, her fingers gripping the rough bark with a determined urgency. She ascended to a sturdy branch, crawling out towards the sky, balancing precariously as she reached out her hand to the distant moon.

"Take it, Lessie. Take my hand," she pleaded, her arm outstretched, as if she could bridge the vast expanse between earth and sky. Her lonely figure silhouetted against the moonlit sky, her hand reaching towards an impossible dream. Jerome stood on the brink, her heart full of hope and desperation, her eyes locked on the moon, believing that somehow, some way, Leslie would reach back.

Chapter 24

Kitty set the dishes on the outdoor table, the soft glow of the torches casting flickering shadows across the patio. The air was thick with the scent of the evening's meal, mingled with the faint perfume of the garden flowers. As she arranged the plates, Sterling approached, his steps heavy and uncertain.

Her heart sank at the sight of him—his face pale, blood crusted under his nose, and his clothes stained with spilled wine. He looked utterly disheveled.

"Oh my god, Sterling... What happened?" Kitty's voice was filled with concern as she rushed towards him.

Sterling didn't answer, his eyes glazed over with a distant, haunted look. He slumped into a chair, his body collapsing. The sobs came suddenly, wracking his body with a force that seemed to shatter him from within.

Kitty grabbed a napkin and dipped it into a water glass, her hands trembling. She knelt beside him, cradling his head in her arms, the napkin dabbing gently at the blood on his face. Her touch was tender, filled with a quiet strength that sought to comfort and protect.

"It's okay," she whispered, her voice steady. "No one is going to hurt you. I'm here."

Sterling's sobs intensified, each cry tearing at Kitty's

heart. He seemed so lost, so broken, and she felt an overwhelming need to shelter him from whatever pain he was experiencing.

"I messed up," he choked out between sobs, his voice raw with guilt and despair.

"Shh," Kitty soothed, her own eyes glistening with unshed tears. "It's okay. Everything will be okay."

She held him close, her arms wrapped around him with a fierce protectiveness. In that moment, the world outside seemed to fade away, leaving only the two of them in a fragile bubble of shared sorrow and love. Kitty stroked his hair, whispering reassurances, trying to instill a sense of calm and safety.

As Sterling continued to cry, Kitty felt her own emotions swell, a mix of empathy, sadness, and a deep, abiding love. She wished she could take away his pain, erase whatever had led him to this point, but all she could do was be there for him, offering her support and unconditional love.

Chapter 25

Marybelle sat in front of her mirror, her reflection staring back with a mix of uncertainty and self-critique. She wiped off the last traces of makeup, revealing her bare face, unadorned and vulnerable. As she did, Max entered the room, his gaze softening as he took in her natural appearance.

"You're beautiful just like that," he murmured, his voice gentle and reassuring. "I like you natural."

Marybelle frowned slightly, her fingers tracing the outline of her lips. "Oh, Max. My eyes disappear and my lips are too thin."

Max shook his head, his eyes meeting hers in the mirror. "I don't like the paint," he said simply, his tone filled with sincerity.

She sighed, her shoulders slumping. "The gals are always so perfect. I have to be more like that. More... Together or with it, I guess. I'm such a runt."

Max patted the bed beside him, beckoning her over. "Belle... Come here."

She moved over, sitting beside him, her hands nervously fidgeting in her lap. Max took a deep breath, his expression thoughtful. "I've been thinking. Um, maybe it's time that we try to have a baby."

Marybelle's eyes widened, a flicker of hope and fear crossing her face. "Oh Max... I'd love it... But I still don't have my makeup right and I'd have to get a whole new wardrobe and this house... This is our house, not a house for a baby..."

Max gently placed a hand on her cheek, turning her to face him. "Shhhh. Belle, look at me. You are beautiful. I don't care about the other stuff. I think we should move. Start over again."

"Move? Away from our friends?" she asked, her voice tinged with hesitation.

"Away from everyone," he replied firmly.

Marybelle blinked, tears welling up in her eyes. "Yes, Max, yes. Another house. We could buy a house for a family. I could make sure the colors were right, soothing colors and we could put a swing set in the back and somewhere that's got grass and real trees..."

Max smiled, pulling her into a hug. "Colorado. We can move to the mountains. Live on our own, away from people."

A tear rolled down her cheek as she clung to him. "Yes, yes, yes. I could just slide out of bed in the morning and pull my hair back into a ponytail and make pancakes..."

Max held her tightly, his voice filled with quiet conviction. "Belle, I want to. I want to."

She exhaled deeply, her grip on him tightening as if afraid he might disappear. A small, tentative smile formed on her lips, a glimmer of freedom in her eyes. "And no mirrors, right Max? We can live in a house without mirrors."

Max nodded, brushing a strand of hair from her face. "Yes, Belle-Belle. We can live without all that stuff."

Marybelle's eyes brightened with a mix of relief and determination. "I'm afraid, Max. Everyone's always looking. They're always looking at me."

Max gently stroked her back, his voice soothing. "The only neighbors we'll have are the deer and the squirrels."

Something shifted inside Marybelle, a spark igniting in her eyes. She jumped up, pulling Max towards her vanity. "Max, help me, I'm scared. Help me."

She looked at herself in the mirror, then at Max, her reflection a mix of anxiety and hope. In a burst of defiance, she swept all the makeup off the table, sending it crashing to the floor. "More, Max. More, more..."

They moved to the closet, tearing through the clothes in a frenzy of liberation. Dresses, suits, everything was ripped apart, their laughter echoing through the room. The act was cathartic, a release of pent-up emotions and insecurities.

Finally, they collapsed onto the pile of shredded clothing, their bodies entwined, breathing heavily. In that moment, Marybelle felt a weight lift from her shoulders, a sense of liberation washing over her. She looked into Max's eyes, seeing the same mix of fear and excitement reflected back at her.

As they lay there, the remnants of their past scattered around them, Marybelle felt a flicker of hope, a tentative belief that they could truly start over, free from the pressures and expectations that had weighed them down for so long.

Chapter 26

Burt and Florene reached orgasm at the same time. He rolled off her to the side and they lay intertwined, basking in the afterglow. Their breaths were heavy, mingling with the soft rustle of the sheets. The room felt charged with the warmth of rekindled affection and the quiet satisfaction of a love reaffirmed. Burt's hand traced the contours of Florene's face, his eyes reflecting a tender adoration.

"I love you, wife," Burt whispered, his voice deep and sincere.

Florene smiled, her eyes shimmering with a mix of joy and tears. "I love you, husband," she responded, her voice soft but firm. They leaned in, sharing a kiss that was gentle.

Burt reached for the remote and turned on the television, filling the room with the soft glow of the screen. They settled back, their attention captured by the broadcast. The iconic images of the moon landing filled the screen, a scene of historic significance that mirrored their own moment of clarity and renewal.

"Ladies and Gentlemen, let's repeat the week's exceptional news, the most significant event in the history of mankind," the commentator's voice narrated, setting the tone for the monumental moment.

The words of Neil Armstrong echoed through the speakers, each syllable etched into the annals of history. "I am going to step off the landing. It's one small step for man, one giant leap for mankind."

Florene, her eyes wide with awe, adjusted her glasses, her gaze fixed on the screen. "Jesus H. Christ!" she exclaimed, her voice a mixture of reverence and disbelief.

Burt, equally astonished, echoed her sentiment, "Holy shit."

The phone rang, momentarily pulling them from their reverie. Burt grabbed it, his eyes never leaving the screen. "Yeah, we're watching it! How did we miss this the first time? Unfuckingbelievable," he said, shaking his head in wonder.

As they continued to watch, Armstrong's voice described the lunar landscape with a quiet awe. "It has a stark beauty all its own. It's like much of the high desert of the United States. It's different, but it's very pretty out here. Are you getting a picture now, Houston?"

The response from Houston came, filled with pride and excitement. "Neil, yes we are getting a picture. You're gonna fill the view now."

Florene and Burt turned up the volume, their faces illuminated by the glow of the screen. The stark, alien beauty of the lunar surface stretched before them, a symbol of human achievement and the limitless possibilities of exploration.

Buzz Aldrin's voice, filled with wonder, came through the speakers. "Beautiful view!"

Armstrong responded, his voice carrying a profound sense of discovery and admiration. "Isn't that something!

Magnificent sight out here."

The room fell silent, the only sound the faint hum of the television. Florene and Burt were transfixed, their thoughts far removed from their daily lives, lost in the vastness of space and the shared experience of humanity reaching beyond its bounds.

Burt felt a lump form in his throat, a mix of pride and melancholy welling up inside him. The sight of the moon, distant yet so profoundly connected to human history and dreams, stirred something deep within. It was a moment of clarity, a reminder of the fragility of life and the boundless potential of the human spirit.

Florene squeezed Burt's hand, her grip firm and reassuring. They exchanged a glance, one that spoke of shared memories and unspoken dreams. In that moment, the trivialities and troubles of their lives seemed to fade away, replaced by a deep sense of unity and purpose.

Finally, Aldrin's voice broke the silence, his words describing the essence of more than just that moment. "Magnificent desolation."

ABOUT THE AUTHOR

ELLA SPENCER

With a background in literature and a passion for exploring the intricacies of human relationships, Ella's love for travel and adventure often finds its way into her novels, bringing vibrant settings to life and adding an extra layer of enchantment to her tales.

When she's not writing, Ella enjoys exploring new cultures, savoring exotic cuisines, and spending time with her beloved family. She currently resides in a charming coastal town, where she continues to dream up new stories that celebrate the beauty of love in all its forms.

More titles from Ella Spencer:

"Venetian Nights of Desire"
Dikenga Books

www.DIKENGA.com